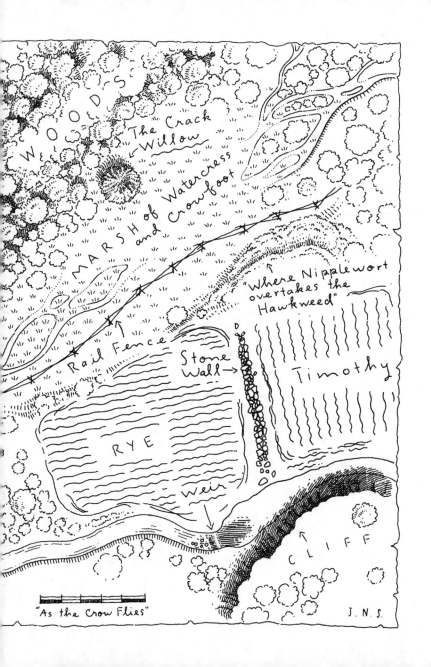

The Linnet's Tale

DALE C. WILLARD

Illustrations by James Noel Smith

SCRIBNER PAPERBACK FICTION
Published by Simon & Schuster
New York   London   Toronto   Sydney   Singapore

SCRIBNER PAPERBACK FICTION
Simon & Schuster, Inc.
Rockefeller Center
1230 Avenue of the Americas
New York, NY 10020

First Scribner Paperback Fiction edition 2002
SCRIBNER PAPERBACK FICTION and design are trademarks of Macmillan Library
Reference USA, Inc., used under license by Simon & Schuster,
the publisher of this work.

For information regarding special discounts for bulk purchases,
please contact Simon & Schuster Special Sales at 1-800-456-6798 or
business@simonandschuster.com

DESIGNED BY ERICH HOBBING

Manufactured in the United States of America

1   3   5   7   9   10   8   6   4   2

Library of Congress Cataloging-in-Publication Data is available.

ISBN 0-7432-2498-1 (Pbk)

For Stuart and Emily

ACKNOWLEDGMENTS

No one makes a book alone. To those who helped me with this one, I'm very grateful:

—to my family—Myra, Stephanie, Cecily and Cameron—for strong encouragements, great suggestions and gentle critiques;

—to Mike Cole, who named this book and whose ideas and sense of fun are such a part of it;

—to Mara Sidmore, whose insights helped to jump-start a stalled project;

—to Kristine Puopolo, who taught me what a talented and hardworking editor can do for a manuscript;

—to Todd Keithley, for his faith in the book and for his skill and savvy in finding a place for it;

—to David Forbes, for so much generous and enthusiastic technical help;

—to Bill and Beverly Martin, for early encouragement and good advice;

—to Caroline Sutton and Nicole Diamond, to Stacey Glick and to Jennifer Reilly, for all their cheerful and expert support;

—and, not least, to Jeff Willard, who reminded me at the right moment that this is, after all, a story for grown-ups.

CONTENTS

The Linnet's Tale

PROLOGUE

I am, of course, a bird. That is beyond dispute. And though some Americans will call me a house finch, I suppose, until the day they perish from the earth, I should like *you* to know, at the beginning of things, that I refer to myself as a linnet.

Small difference, you might say. House finch. Linnet.

Perhaps. Still, would you be called a house finch if it were in your power to be known as a linnet? No, I thought not. Nevertheless, let's be good friends—whatever you may call me—and, though I did wish you to know my position, I shall not bring this matter up again.

And now to my purpose. I should like to tell you about a delightful company of field mice who once lived in a place called Tottensea Burrows and how it came to happen that they all went away. I can only hope that sounds interesting to you. It was certainly interesting to me. But, of course, it would be, wouldn't it?

I was not fully fledged when I discovered the mice of Tottensea Burrows—or, rather, when they discovered me. That was before Langston Pickerel came to them and *well* before they knew who he was. But then Mr. Neversmythe came to Mrs. Pockets in the rain and began asking questions about the Saracen dagger. Still, we can't blame Mr. Neversmythe for the way things turned out. And, technically, we can't even blame Langston Pickerel. Technically, it was poor little unthinking Harrington Doubletooth who brought everything down around their ears!

I do hope this is clear. What I'm trying to say is that none of them had the faintest notion there were pirates about. Even less did they expect to be running for their lives from something MUCH WORSE than pirates. But, in the end, they were pleased about it, you see. Running for their lives, I mean. The mice.

Blast! I seem to be mucking this up. It's entirely possible you haven't the slightest idea what I'm talking about. I must try to repair. Let us make a beginning, then, with the geography of things. "Where, after all, *is* this Tottensea Burrows?" you might ask. Very well. Here:

If you're the sort of creature who keeps to roads and lanes and that kind of business, here is what you must do to reach Tottensea Burrows. From Dollopsford, go toward Lesser Triffleton. Left at the New Road, past Nubbins-on-Stith and left again. If you find yourself at something called Doxmere at the Stoke, you've gone completely wrong and I can only advise you to retrace your path immediately. Say nothing to anyone. Try again in the morning. Otherwise, straight on, watching for a stone cottage with one or two small structures off to the side and a beech tree and some hollyhocks. Tottensea Burrows is there. In the rear.

If you are winged, of course, it's much simpler. Begin at that field of rye beside the weir below those rocks under that cliff overlooking the stone wall which is berried over in the early autumn. You know the place I mean. Fly straight above that patch of timothy next it, wheel to the left just where nipplewort overtakes the hawkweed and on to the rail fence running through that marsh of watercress and crowfoot. Rest a bit in the crack willow, lift over the wood and, right where the hazels leave off, dive 'twixt the two elms, and stop in the beech tree beyond the slate roof. Tottensea Burrows is there. In the rear. As I said.

And it *is* still there, of course. Boarded up and abandoned it may be and all its inhabitants happily away to where they belong, but if you were of a mind to do it, you could, with no special equipment and simply by creeping about in the right places, see all kinds of interesting things there, even now. (Careful of your step, of course—the more especially if you happen to be of the larger bipedal type.)

In the lee of that rock sticking up out of the lyme grass one could still find the mossy green roof of The Bookish Mouse, I expect. And under its eaves could be seen the little row of mullioned windows which enabled the bookshop's customers to browse its volumes in glorious daylight, careless of candles and lanterns, and with both paws free, therefore, to riffle a mousebook's pages if they liked.

And if The Man has not spaded up the dewberries for a patch of runner beans as he so often told The Woman he was about to do, you could, in all likelihood, see the thatched gables of Mrs. Pockets' boardinghouse snugged down in the thicket out there, low and well out of the way of things—though the swinging sign out front that said THE BRAMBLES was somewhat in need of repainting even then. I can't think how it must look now!

If you went amongst the climber vines—beyond the

clematis, I mean—the part of Swift Mercantile which you could see above the ground would appear so modest and unimpressive that you would have no conception of the vast and sprawling warehouses below. To see them you *would* need a bit of special equipment, I'm afraid. A lantern, say, and a pinch bar of the proper size should do very nicely.

Armed with those, then, you could see more than Swift's warehouses. Indeed, if you poked about the wisteria roots, you might get a look at the workshop of Opportune Baggs The Inventor. There should be many things for you to see. He left in great haste, after all, and he couldn't take everything, could he? There would be hammers and saws, of course, but, beyond all that, there might be some interesting tinkering apparatus down there: little squeezers and stretchers, for example, or crimpers and crinklers—jigglers, even—and some clever little winders and loopers that he thought up one night when he was in bed and almost asleep.

And you should be prepared to see some things in his workshop that you would have no proper idea *what* they were: contrivances for making square objects roundish, perhaps, or round objects squarish or both of them odd-shaped. Who knows? I've been down there. I saw some very shrewd devices to hold things together and some even shrewder ones to keep them apart. There were implements for smoothing and others for roughing up. He had an appliance over here to straighten a piece out and one over there to make it crooked! Whatever he thought best, you see. It depended.

If you wanted to try out things, his treadle lathe would turn as freely as ever, I expect, and the bow drill make quite a reasonable hole in whatever scrap of stock he might have left lying about for one to be fooling with. But you mustn't think you could try the Mousewriter, of course. It isn't there.

Down the way and under the hydrangea, you could peep inside The Silver Claw, if you liked. It wouldn't be the same lively place one remembers, you understand. No one would clap you on the back and offer refreshment. There'd be no tales of wonderful deeds, no one to speak of Warburton Nines Who Once Lifted A Cat, say, or Merchanty Swift Who Brought The Cheese Trade Down To Earth Almost Single-Handedly. Nothing like that. The chairs would be up on tables, I expect, and all the lanterns out. Still, with the lantern you brought with you, you could see the dartboard if you wished and what was left of the flowers on the mantel shelf—dry as sticks, certainly, if they were there at all. The kettle behind the counter would be quiet and still and everything covered with an inch of dust, as they say. (Not an actual inch, of course—a mouseinch, more like.)

Every one of these places, in fact, would now be as quiet and still as The Silver Claw's kettle and covered with dust in its own right. But there was a time, and not so long ago, when Tottensea Burrows was athrive and bustling with this quite splendid little company of field mice—all of them honorable, generous, warmhearted and as distinct from one another as snowflakes. You'd like them, I think.

CHAPTER 1

Grenadine Learns the Language

Grenadine Fieldpea used to conjugate field mouse verbs, aloud, while sitting at the breakfast table, swinging her legs under the chair and waiting for her mother to finish boiling the oatmeal. It sounded like this:

> *I will eat porridge*
> *you will eat porridge*
> *he will eat porridge*
>
> *we will eat porridge*
> *you will eat porridge*
> *they will eat porridge*
>
> *I will be eating porridge*
> *you will be eating porridge*
> *And so on.*

Grenadine's sisters, Almandine and Incarnadine, would beg their mother to make her stop doing this and, indeed, at some point—as no one could likely parse an entire field

21

mouse verb before breakfast!—her mother would be forced to do exactly that, saying something like "Stop conjugating, Grenadine, and eat your porridge. It's getting quite cold. And besides, dear, you've got the future perfect progressive all in a muddle. It's 'I will have been eating' not 'I will have been having eaten.'"

Grenadine was, all her life, a quite linguistic mouse. But when she was little, this characteristic tended toward extremes. At one point, for example, when her interest had turned a little away from conjugating verbs and more toward acquiring vocabulary, she began to run across words in the dictionary that she thought very fine and that needed to be more evident in field mouse usage. She thereupon under-took, herself, a small crusade to this end. The first method she tried was simply to quote the definition of the words to everyone, in turn, giving full particulars, and at the end, an exhortation. Mr. and Mrs. Fieldpea found it pleasant enough to be accosted a few times a day by a small mouse holding a large book who would read out something like:

SIMULTANEOUS adjective: existing or occurring at the same time. See COINCIDENT

followed by "Please use that as soon as possible." Or

SUBSEQUENT adjective: following in time, order, or place. See SUCCEEDING.

"Before lunch, if you can. Thanks."

Almandine found this less pleasant than her parents did

and would often say, "Oh, Grenadine, stop!" while Incarnadine, finding it less pleasant still, might respond with something more along the lines of "Go away. See LEAVE."

At length, Grenadine abandoned the first method because it didn't seem to her to be doing any good. Although Mr. Fieldpea would often try to help out at meals with "I shall have some of that gooseberry jam SIMULTANEOUSLY with my toast, please," or "I noticed some STRIATIONS today— lengthwise, along a stick," and Mrs. Fieldpea would respond with "How PICTURESQUE that must have been," Grenadine's sisters were not being improved in any lexical respect that she could observe. Whatsoever!

Her second method was to ply her chosen word in every conversation one could conceivably work it into—thus to teach by example. This was sometimes more difficult than others, of course, depending on the word. It was no trouble at all to find ways to use a word like "ingenious." Everything in the Fieldpea burrow simply became ingenious. Its floor was an ingenious floor, its walls were ingenious walls, and it had an ingenious candlestick which held an ingenious candle. But contorting ordinary conversation into something that could accommodate casual references to a word like "proteinaceous," on the other hand, became an awful thing indeed.

For some reason not well understood, Grenadine got quite insistent about this particular word and let it be known that, although she was getting no help whatsoever in her effort to raise PROTEINACEOUS up, they would all of them do well to get on with it as she was not going to permit the DEMISE of attention to this poor word, allowing it, therefore, to be RELEGATED to its customary OBSCURITY—"demise" and "obscurity" being words from the previous day and "relegate" from one or two days before that.

"Proteinaceous," then, provoked a crisis.

But Grenadine was lucky in mothers, having got one who was wise and loving and who knew a thing or two about words, herself. When the search for protein references began to threaten with tension—if not tears—almost every Fieldpea conversation in which Grenadine was involved, her mother said to her, "Try '*pert*inacious' dear. It sounds almost as good and it's much easier. It means perversely persistent; stubbornly unyielding or tenacious. See OBSTINATE. Try using it right away, then." And though Grenadine said she couldn't think of a way to work that in, everyone noticed the SUBSEQUENT DEMISE of the vocabulary crusade.

Mr. and Mrs. Fieldpea cheered up a bit when Grenadine turned to poetry. "Ah, sweet poesy," they thought to themselves. Here would be something less technical—more flowing and generous. But then they remembered that versification can be quite rigorous. Then they remembered, with increasing unease, that, in fact, it absolutely bristles with mechanical aspects. Grenadine found these right away.

The study of meter she liked very much. She could be heard around the burrow explaining metrical things to others: "Ta-TUM ta-TUM ta-TUM. That's iambic, you see, ta-TUM being an iamb. TUM-ta, on the other hand, is a trochee. Whereas an anapest . . ."

What was additionally trying was that she would point out interesting features of one's meter in conversation. If Almandine were to say to her, "Why are you wearing that old dress?" Grenadine might respond with, "That's two dactyls and a spondee, Almandine!" And if Almandine, in turn, said something back like "Will you stop doing that every time I say something!" Grenadine would probably observe that that line contained a molossus in the first foot.

As bad as Grenadine's meter period was, however, the rhyming period was worse. It started with something like "Grenadine, it's time for tea" being answered by "That is such good news to me," or "It's your turn to clean the room" by "You were told that, dear, by whom?"—harmless enough, one might think. But I assure you that such a practice, continued indefinitely, is very likely to provoke irritation—in sisters, for example. Now I think of it, especially in sisters.

When Almandine's

I can't find my other sock

was answered by Grenadine's

Have you looked beneath that rock?

Almandine would ask, of course, "What rock?"

Grenadine, searching less for the sock than for some decent rhymes, would reply,

Or, if a rock cannot be found
then try the other way around.

Almandine, then, who, in her childhood, tended more toward literal thinking and less toward the poetical, would turn around!

This would move Grenadine to say,

> *No, no! Please exercise your wit*
> *If there's no sock*
> *beneath the rock*
> *Perhaps the rock is under it.*

"What rock?" Almandine would reply. "There's no rock!" Grenadine, by now having completely lost interest in the rock, it having served its purpose in the scheme of rhymes, would move on to other aspects of the problem at hand:

> *If one were careful with one's clothes*
> *one shouldn't lose them, I suppose.*

This last couplet would be lost on Almandine, however, who, by this time, would be on her way to the kitchen to ask her mother to make Grenadine stop saying there was a rock when there most certainly WASN'T ONE!

Mrs. Fieldpea became increasingly worried about Grenadine's excesses and their effect on family life. While realizing that her daughter might have some talent in things linguistic and might well, indeed, have a future in the field, the incessant squabbling and chaos which this talent was now causing, conjoined with the social obtuseness—and blank obstinacy!—of Grenadine, herself, was distressing to her.

She would sometimes discuss the matter with Mr. Fieldpea in the evenings.

"What shall we do about Grenadine, dear?" she might say, over her needlepoint—the figure of a large crimson radish stitched upon a ground of pale amber.

"Hmm. Grenadine," Mr. Fieldpea would probably reply. But he might say it very slowly while not putting his newspaper down from in front of his face quite as promptly as Mrs. Fieldpea would have liked. She, however, would overlook this, for reasons which I shall presently explain. At length, he would put his newspaper down, of course, and then, with an expression on his face not unlike that of a mouse awakened from a deep sleep, he would blink one or two times, and, with admirable determination, focus his eyes directly upon Mrs. Fieldpea, who—he would then realize—was sitting in a chair right there in the room with him! Having focused, he would say, as if he were trying to recall something, "What shall we do about Grenadine?" This would be followed by a brief pause after which he would say, "Yes."

Mrs. Fieldpea, not looking up from the radish, would then notice, pleasantly, that Mr. Fieldpea had joined her on the very same planet which she was now inhabiting. But I must hasten to say that, very far from being irritated by this slight delay in her husband's response, she had learned to be flattered by it. Now, let me see if I can explain that.

Mrs. Fieldpea, you see, knew that her husband was not inclined to think about several things at once, as she was like to do. Mr. Fieldpea thought about one thing at a time. But he thought VERY DEEPLY. And she considered that he did it exceedingly well. In fact, Mrs. Fieldpea thought this inclination to deep thinking somewhat superior to her own. I, personally, am not at all sure that it was superior. But she thought it so and I count that rather splendid—for her to think that, I mean—the more so since he had always admired her for her ability to move effortlessly from one necessary line of thought to another.

In any event, Mrs. Fieldpea knew that for Mr. Fieldpea to leave off thinking about what he was reading in his newspaper in order to attend to what she was asking him to think about at that moment required a certain deliberate adjustment of his interior processes. And she felt . . . well, rather honored that he undertook such an effort for her, if you see what I mean. But it did require a small space of time, that adjustment.

One evening—after such an adjustment—Mr. Fieldpea said, "I've been thinking about Grenadine and the others, as a matter of fact. Today, actually."

"Really?" said Mrs. Fieldpea, interested.

"Yes," he continued. "It occurred to me that siblings are very useful to one another. It's as if one were to rattle small stones about in a box until they were all of them quite smooth. Do you think that reasonable?"

"Yes, I believe I do," she said.

He went on. "It's quite wonderful in its effect—this rattling about—but it does, at times, set up something of a small racket, you see."

"Hmm. Yes. Of course it would," she said, frowning thoughtfully. "We simply will have a *bit* of noise, then."

"A bit, yes. But only within reasonable limits," he

emphasized, picking up his newspaper. Then he put it back down and added this thought: "So we mustn't give up hope, I think."

"No. Certainly not," said Mrs. Fieldpea, just putting the last crimson stitch in the tip of the radish near the very bottom edge of the lovely amber ground.

And generally they don't. Give up hope, I mean. Field mice.

Neither do they, as parents, moreover, leave all the smoothing to the other small stones. When one day, Mr. Fieldpea said:

"Grenadine, enough of this rhyming business for now!" and his daughter answered with:

"Do you mean a rough amiss timing is this somehow?" (which, if one works it out, was quite remarkable, but *very* disobedient)—it cost her some desserts.

Being rhymed at by a small tenacious field mouse will not, of course, cause anyone actual physical harm. Disobedience, however, will cause all manner of harm to that small tenacious field mouse, herself—and Mr. and Mrs. Fieldpea knew it. All considerations of Grenadine's talent or future had to be put aside until this issue of minding one's parents could be settled. It took a bit of their own tenacity for her mother and father *to* settle it, but, at length, it *was* settled. And due to such settling, Grenadine grew up a happier mouse— easier to live with, and much better liked by her sisters. In fact, as they came of age, the Fieldpea girls were known in Tottensea Burrows not only for being beautiful and accomplished, but also for being practically inseparable.

CHAPTER 2

Tea at The Bookish Mouse

Close by the Fieldpea front door you would find, off to your right, the entrance to The Bookish Mouse—Tottensea Burrows' finest mousebook shop. It was a restful and inviting place, with a few overstuffed chairs, well broken in and scattered about in pairs, so that one might sit and discuss with a friend the merits of a work or the advisability of its purchase. There were bookshelves right up the walls of The Bookish Mouse, and, in the middle, islands of shelves, though not so tall as all that, certainly taller than the average mouse. It was, on the whole, an agreeably clean shop though not every volume and every shelf was always and completely above having a bit of dust along the tops of them, you understand. It had a varnished wooden floor which was worn white in certain places from being walked on and which squeaked pleasantly as you moved about among the books that interested you.

Mr. Glendowner Fieldpea was the proprietor of The Bookish Mouse, and he normally sat on a tall stool at the little carved cherry wood counter by the door where customers would come to pay for their purchases or to ask questions. It was, not uncommonly, a quiet shop in the early hours of business and, in fact, the squeaking of the floor, the riffling of pages and the necessary clearing of a mouse's throat, from time to time, might be all there was to be heard in the place for half a morning. Owing to the general quietness at such times and to the occasional want of fresh air in The Bookish Mouse, its proprietor was once or twice discovered to be precariously asleep atop his tall three-legged stool. But only once or twice, as I say, and, in all fairness, things being as they were, it could have happened to almost anyone.

But if slow in the mornings, business at The Bookish Mouse was predictably brisk at teatime. For it was then that Mrs. Emmalina Fieldpea would spread a crisp white cloth on the little round table next to Contemporary Rodent Fiction and offer to their customers her traditional refreshment of acorn butter and blackthorn jam on oat-seed cakes along with a cup of piping hot black India tea. Indeed, so celebrated were these delicious comestibles that about four o'clock in the afternoon various of the Tottensea mice might be asking themselves if perhaps they really shouldn't go and have a look at that book they had been thinking of buy-ing, fully realizing at that particular time of day that, after all, a mouse mustn't *always* be putting off a thing that needed doing.

Having tea at The Bookish Mouse was one of the finest things to be done in all Tottensea Burrows and you may be sure that no mice doing it were ever heard to say anything tiresome about the dangers of mixing business with pleasure. Pleasure was exactly what they wanted mixed into the business of buying their books. Clementine Nickelpenny, for example, came to tea one afternoon seeking romance. And who would deny her a bit of pleasure in business like that? Certainly not the mice. And when, over her cake, Mrs. Nickelpenny told Mrs. Fieldpea of her mission, Mrs. Fieldpea summoned her daughters.

The three Fieldpea daughters had grown up with books, of course, and so they were wonderfully helpful in the bookshop. If you wanted a mousebook but didn't know exactly which mousebook, and if Emmalina and Glendowner were busy serving tea or making change, then you would talk to Grenadine about it. Or to Almandine. Or to Incarnadine. Or, in weighty matters such as romance, you might talk to all three of them at once.

"Hmm." Grenadine said, upon hearing Mrs. Nickelpenny's request. After a little thought, she turned to her sisters. "Perhaps she might enjoy *Love at the Brink*?"

"Yes," Almandine said, rubbing her chin, "I like that book but, I wonder . . ."

"What would you think of *Come Away, Mouse*?" Incarnadine asked.

"Oh, dear!" Grenadine said. Then to Mrs. Nickelpenny: "Do you like excitement?"

"Well, it depends, doesn't it?" Mrs. Nickelpenny said, blinking and placing a paw at her throat.

"Ah! I have it!" Almandine said. "The very book." At that, she climbed a little way up a ladder and, after a brief search, drew out a book and handed it down to their customer.

"*Millicent's Surprised Heart,*" Mrs. Nickelpenny read the title aloud.

"Perfect!" said Incarnadine. "Just the thing. Bra*vo,* Almandine."

But Grenadine was cautious. "Do you fancy crying over stories?"

"I do, actually," Mrs. Nickelpenny said, and blushed.

"Then there's your book!" Grenadine said, beaming with satisfaction.

"If all comes right in the end, of course," Mrs. Nickelpenny added, on second thought.

"Well, I mustn't tell you the ending!" Grenadine said. Then with a smile she leaned toward Mrs. Nickelpenny and whispered, "But you'll be very pleased, I think."

Just then, Opportune Baggs The Inventor came into The Bookish Mouse wearing more different plaids at the same time than he should have. He tended to accumulate plaids through the day—Opportune Baggs did—as the temperature varied in his workshop. If he started out in his blue-and-white-plaid shirt, say, and a chill crept over the workshop, he might just slip on his black-and-green-plaid jerkin for comfort and then, if he went out, he might add his red-and-yellow-plaid cap to the blend. And though his plaids were separately attractive, taken altogether they appeared to be rather in dispute.

On this day Opportune Baggs, being somewhat preoccupied, had come to The Bookish Mouse directly *from* the workshop without having passed through the kitchen on his way, where Mrs. Baggs would have normally—and in the nicest sort of way—brought such things as a confusion of plaids to his notice. So he certainly had no intention to offend in his plaids, it's just that on this particular day he was preoccupied, as I say, and the thing he was preoccupied *with* was the hypotenuse.

At The Bookish Mouse tea table, he spoke to Mrs. Fieldpea about the hypotenuse. "That would be Incarnadine," Mrs. Fieldpea said and waved a paw over her head to engage her daughter's attention in the busy room. When Incarnadine had come and been told of the problem she asked Mr. Baggs what were his specific requirements for a book about the hypotenuse.

"Something an untrained mouse could understand," he said.

"Of course," she said. "It's all about triangles isn't it? Let's see what we can find." And off they went to the mouse-science section.

At that moment, Almandine was being asked by Mr. Adverbial Quoty for something practical on poetry and General Random Chewings was inquiring of Grenadine if there were anything available on fusiliers.

"Practical. Poetry. Hmm," Almandine said to Adverbial Quoty. "Now there are two words I've never used in the same thought!"

"Fusiliers," Grenadine said to General Chewings. "I'm afraid you must first tell me what fusiliers *are,* General."

While these conversations were going forward, a mouse named Merchanty Swift came into the bookshop.

The appearance of Merchanty Swift in The Bookish Mouse wrought a certain noticeable effect upon Grenadine, Almandine and Incarnadine. They all looked at one another, significantly, felt suddenly warm and began to be slightly flustered. Almandine actually fanned herself.

"Yes, well, fusils are muskets, aren't they?" the General was saying to Grenadine as she watched Merchanty Swift spread the acorn butter across his oat-seed cake in a remarkably debonair way, she thought. "Fusiliers, then, you see, would be those units which are furnished with fusils . . ."

Almandine was straining to see if Merchanty Swift took sugar when Adverbial Quoty at just the wrong time put a difficult passage from Mr. T. S. Eliot right in front of her, making her view of Merchanty Swift, at that moment, as obscure to her as Mr. T. S. Eliot's poetry was to Adverbial Quoty.

Incarnadine was hoping that Opportune Baggs might agree quickly that the little gray text entitled *Triangles and Things* was just what he wanted so that she might then be free to go and help a certain handsome other customer across the room who seemed in imminent danger of finishing his refreshments and leaving The Bookish Mouse straightaway. But, just as Mr. Baggs was about to make his decision, he was distracted. Indeed, every mouse in the room was distracted!

A lemming had just come into The Bookish Mouse. And not only a lemming but a lemming who stood for some few moments, just inside the doorway, looking awkward and uncomfortable and somewhat sinister. When he saw that all eyes were upon him, the lemming abruptly snatched a book from the nearest shelf and pretended to take an interest in it. But any mouse who watched saw that he was looking right over the tops of the book's pages and was, in fact, searching the face of every creature in The Bookish Mouse.

After he had his look at everyone, the lemming stuffed his pockets with tea cakes and left without saying a word. And he was not to be seen again by the mice, that lemming, until he returned to Tottensea Burrows late one night in a drenching rainstorm.

Soon after the lemming left, Merchanty Swift, apparently having finished his business—or at least his refreshments—left as well. Grenadine's, Almandine's and Incarnadine's hearts settled down a little and they went on with *their* business.

In the end, Opportune Baggs took *Triangles and Things* on approval. General Random Chewings left off looking for books about fusiliers and had a cup of tea, instead. Adverbial Quoty sat for quite a long time by himself in an overstuffed chair reading bravely at a poem called "A Cooking Egg" until, giving up on it utterly, he bought himself a reasonably portable rhyming dictionary and went out.

Mrs. Nickelpenny had to go right home from The Bookish Mouse to start Merchanty Swift's dinner. But later, after the washing up, she retired to her rooms, got into bed and, as was her habit, read until she fell asleep—somewhere after the part where Millicent had been orphaned and sent away to the workhouse.

CHAPTER 3

An Evening with the Baggses

Opportune Baggs The Inventor was much more than an inventor. In fact, there were those who said he was a renaissance mouse and, in a way, I suppose he was, though certainly not a commercially successful renaissance mouse—whatever kind of thing that would be. But he was definitely more than an inventor. He had, in fact, an entire galaxy of careers—so many that it became an embarrassment for him to iterate them all and it was this embarrassment which made him content when the word "inventor" became attached to his name. Inventing was not any more successful than his other careers, but it had this advantage: it was one thing, inventing, and not an entire list of things. So it was to be hoped that when mice asked him at picnics and cotillions and things what it was that he did—and some mice incessantly want to know what it is you *do*—and he replied that he was an inventor, those mice would then be able to imagine him doing that one thing and *not* hopping about from book writing to picture painting to manufacturing speculative products to delivering newspapers and things like that. And, if one thinks about it, "inventing" turns out to be a word that can actually apply to almost everything he did—writing, painting and manufacturing, certainly, and, obviously enough, inventing.

But I wouldn't have you think the mouse a failure. He made some inventions that actually worked. Once, for example, having passed a bad afternoon—on a Tuesday—smashing whortleberries for Mrs. Baggs' jam in several impractical ways, he invented—on a Wednesday—a nifty little appliance which answered to a previously unrecognized need in the field mouse kitchen. And, though not exactly a gold mine, the Baggs Crankable Whortleberry Reducer did bring in the odd mouseshilling from time to time.

In addition, he had a few pieces of fiction in print and at the time of these events had great hope for a small humorous book about humans which he had got up and which he thought might find some acceptance among field mice at least. He had first sent it to a human publishing company called Little, Brown. When they didn't want it he sent it off to Slightly Smaller Than Average, Pink. They didn't care for it either, and so he tried just one more time at Large, Garish Yellow, but, unhappily, they rejected it as well. Giving up on human publication, then, he packed the thing off to

Berries go in there

Mashed-up whortleberries

Juice

RodentHouse, who snapped it up immediately and made quite a respectable little mousebook out of it.

He also placed a piece of poetry, occasionally, through the mails (but poetry doesn't pay *any*thing, even among humans) and he sold paintings at fairs and bazaars (his pieces were, on the whole, I would say, in the Impressionist style) but, by and large, he was not hugely successful at any of the business kinds of things he did.

So, though almost never in despair, Opportune Baggs The Inventor often needed encouragement. And, as so often happens (among field mice, at least), the one mouse in the whole world who most loved to help and encourage Opportune Baggs was actually a member of his own mousehold.

Octavia Baggs was a wonderful mousewife who cheerfully did all sorts of things to help out with expenses while her husband was doing his inventions and books and paintings and things. She did some extra sewing here and there, she gave fipple flute lessons, she catered a picnic or two and she also helped out in a clerical sort of way down at Berryseed Investments when they needed an extra paw. All these things she did, of course, while also minding the children, keeping burrow and doing the shopping, not to mention providing various support services to Mr. Baggs, himself—things like helping him mix his paints (he was slightly color-blind) or copying out his manuscripts so a mouse could read them. And, about that, Mr. Baggs' penmanship left so much to be desired that he would sometimes say to Mrs. Baggs, as he handed her his latest composition for her opinion, "Sorry, dear."

She would then sit down to read the new piece and from

time to time would say something like "Excuse me, darling, this word . . . is it 'figwort' or 'toadflax,' I can't quite . . ."

Mr. Baggs would then look over her shoulder at the errant bit of penmanship. "Hmm," he would say. "Well might you wonder. It's neither, actually. It's 'horse nettle' I'm afraid."

At that point she would say something generous, such as "Oh yes, I can see, now, that it *is* 'horse nettle.' Something about the 'h' led me off, I think." She would then sometimes add, gently, "If only you had a Mousewriter."

That would normally be followed by a sigh from Mr. Baggs, after which he would say, wistfully, "Ah, if only *any*-one had a Mousewriter."

And there is more to say about Octavia Baggs. She was an excellent conversationalist, quite well read-up on things, with very good tastes in literature and a keen eye for flower arranging. A warm and tenderhearted mouse with an attractive sense of humor, she was wise in counsel, saw often to the pith of things and had no tolerance whatsoever for pretense or sophistry of any type. She was, as her husband told me, near as any mouse could get to the perfect wife (though she may have had a *slight* tendency, he said, to throw away things which he might need later).

She also won at gin rummy. Embarrassingly often. And she could cook!

I well remember one occasion at the Baggses' table when she served a mighty aubergine au gratin with a garnish of fresh basil and buttery onion. This was preceded by pumpkin soup and followed by mulberry sundaes, which the chil-

dren loved very much. It was a wonderful time of food and
talk and happiness followed by a bedtime ritual which I
must describe to you in some detail.

While Opportune Baggs and I helped Mrs. Baggs with
the washing up, the children got on their pajamas and gathered expectantly around their father's chair in the sitting
room. As he took his place in their midst, Papa Baggs said,
"So what shall it be tonight, then, darlings? A bit of poetry,
perhaps? Something elevating."

"*Greystreak,* please," piped a small clear voice somewhere
near the front.

"What? *Greystreak* again?"

"Yes, please," said a chorus of mouseling voices all over
the room.

"Didn't we just have that some short time back?"

"Last *night,* Papa, last *night,*" they all said excitedly and
they laughed and some said, "And the night before that,"
while others said "Oh, Papa, you know!" and they all giggled
and giggled and giggled as he took the longest time to polish
his reading spectacles, all the while looking every single one
of them in the eye, in turn. Every single one of them, I do
believe.

"As you wish, then," he said. "*Greystreak* it shall be." A
great cheer went up. He took up the little reddish brown
book which was lying exactly beside the lamp on the table
next to his chair, and one knew, somehow, that there had
never been the slightest doubt about what he was going to
read that evening.

He opened the book and intoned from the title page:

GREYSTREAK
Being a romance
by
Waterford Hopstep
Illustrated

I blushed with pleasure, not at the mention of my name or the name of my book, but at the enjoyment which my book seemed to give these little listeners.

"May we see the frontispiece, please, Papa?"

"Of course," their papa said and turned the book right round and held it up, canting it this way and that so they could all see, in turn, a very average line drawing, partly colored, of a muscular mouse striking something of a heroic pose, looking off somewhere and shading his eyes with a paw.

"May we have the caption, then?"

"Certainly," their papa said and turned the book slightly so as to read, "Greystreak surveys his kingdom." And then, when everyone seemed to be ready—at last—their papa turned the book back round, opened it to the proper page and began to read.

CHAPTER 4

Greystreak

Lord Greystreak was a highborn field mouse and an ento-
mologist. That is to say, he was very rich and it was his
interest to study rare and exotic species of insects wherever
he might have to go to find them. And if one is looking for
rare and exotic species of insects one could do a lot worse
than visiting the back garden out behind the yew hedge.
The soil is very poorly drained back there and, though
the agricultural output is decidedly inferior, there are mar-
velous examples of strange plant life and insect species
such as are yet to be recorded in books. And as Lord
Greystreak *was* very rich and had leisure to do exactly as he
liked, he undertook an extended safari to the back garden
in the heat of summer. Lady Greystreak went with him.
She went with hoopskirts and parasols and, what was
worse, she was expecting.

The heat of summer can be a very bad time for highly
cultured field mice in the back garden, as it turns out, and
so it came to happen that while on this safari Lord and Lady
Greystreak were both of them struck down with the grippe
and thereupon immediately and tragically died. Just before
expiring, however, Lady Greystreak gave birth to one lone

mouseling, a male, small and naked, and seemingly doomed to die right there, wallowing helplessly in a small tussock of fescue. Wonderfully, however, young Greystreak was happened upon by a kind and good family of potato leafhoppers who took him right in, or right up, I should say, into their home at the top of a potato plant where they raised him with tenderness and affection as if he were their own bug.

Owing to this strange upbringing, Greystreak was an unusual mouse in several respects. To begin with the worst, he spoke very poor field mouse. He would out with things like "Greystreak no like eggplant," for example, and other, even stranger locutions which no one had ever imagined. In almost all other respects, however, he was a superb mouse—very noble and good and absolutely overflowing with derring-do of all types.

The leafhoppers taught him their ways and this meant that Greystreak could fairly fly through a thicket of goose-foot, say, covering great distances by swinging from weed to weed and never a paw touching the ground. He also had a mysterious bond with all insect life and was able to communicate with lower creatures by various means, not the least of which was an astonishing and unnerving yell at the top of his lungs which would bring many types of strange multi-legged creatures to his aid wherever he might be.

On one fine afternoon, Greystreak was standing high in a weed surveying his kingdom, as it were, when he suddenly sensed, with his uncanny insectlike sensibilities, that all was not well in the back garden. He swung himself to the ground and stalked through the undergrowth. Creeping through a scrub of henbit and purslane—dotted here and there with a bit of spurge—he came upon an alarming and heartbreaking scene: a coffle of poor house mice, ten or twenty of them, chained hind foot to forepaw and being driven unmercifully by a villainous lot of heavily armed natterjack toads—all of them fitted out in khaki shorts and pith helmets and all of them smoking short cigars. The house mice groaned and strained under enormous loads of spring onions as they moved slowly across a large clearing.

What *on earth* the toads were going to do with all those onions was never determined. Some said they were going to float them down the river on barges and sell them to cats. But that is surely manifest nonsense as cats do not eat spring onions, do they? So we shall have to leave that question pretty much as we found it. And, in any event, it hardly matters what they were going to do with the onions. They had to be stopped.

The stopping itself was a bit more difficult than Greystreak had hoped. Immediately he tried doing it, he found himself surrounded by five armed amphibians with very disagreeable expressions on their faces. He had no alternative, in his own estimation, but to throw back his head and let go the astonishing and unnerving yell at the top of his lungs.

In a matter of moments, there were strange buzzing sounds coming from every direction—starting at a low level and rising steadily to a terrifying frenzy. The toads were then set upon by insects: horseradish flea beetles, raspberry sawflies, turnip aphids and many other things, including at least one clover seed midge—each of them swarming and biting and being generally unpleasant all over the place. Right away, five natterjack toads scattered in five directions with at least one of them coming to a most disagreeable end when a passing goshawk happened to see him and swooped down to catch him away for further disposition at another location—pith helmet and all.

The insects kept coming along well after the toads were gone and the issue decided, until, in fact, the entire clearing was completely filled with a roiling confusion of disorderly arthropods—the lot of them bawling for something to eat or spoiling for a fight or wondering what all this had been about. Greystreak was ever so grateful for their help, of course, but he was having a terrible time of it getting everyone straightened out and sent back home until it suddenly occurred to him what to do—and it turned out to be one of the very best ideas of his career. He simply threw back his head and did the astonishing and unnerving yell at the top of his lungs backwards. There followed a stunned silence in which all the insects in the clearing stood around looking at one another with puzzled expressions. Then, one by one, each creature seemed to realize what he, she or it was supposed to do and did it. The jumble of legs and antennae and proboscises seemed simply to melt away into the surrounding bush—the noise and confusion going with it—until, after a time, everything was completely quiet and the clearing utterly devoid of any insect life, whatsoever.

Greystreak released the poor house mice saying, "You ever no trust natterjack toad again, house mice?" or something like that, and sent them back to the house where they lived a happy life ever after (indoors, I'm afraid, but they didn't seem to mind that, being house mice).

As for Greystreak and his insect friends, they had many further adventures (which are told in other books) and lived contentedly and interestingly, righting wrongs with entomological relish and thoroughness in the vast and trackless wilderness of the back garden for a very long time.

THE END

After the story there was a question.

"What does 'caught him away for further disposition at another location' mean, Papa?" asked a young lady over toward the right and back about halfway.

"It means the goshawk was going to eat him," said one of the boys, quietly.

"Parnassas Baggs," said their papa, "you have it exactly. Eating him is precisely what the goshawk intended to do."

"And did he, then? Eat him, I mean," the young lady asked, concerned.

"Oh, I'm quite certain that he did, my dear Phillipa," said their papa, gravely.

"I hate that, Papa," said Phillipa, in a very small voice.

"I know, my dear," said Opportune Baggs.

CHAPTER 5

A Look at the Drawings

After the children had small milk snacks in the kitchen they returned to the sitting room to take their leave of me. The girls were first. "It was ever so nice to have had you in our home, Mr. Hopstep. We, all of us, enjoy your books exceedingly! I hope you can share another evening with us very soon," said one quite grown-up young lady, accompanying her comment by a lovely smile and a small curtsy. Another one said, "I can't think when I've enjoyed so much having one or another linnet in our home." Still another spoke of "outstanding pleasantness" and "the hope for additional evenings of this type"—she and all of them showing unmistakable flashes of their mother's warmth and hospitality.

The boys, on the other hand, tried more for erudition and vocabulary. "Quite a nice parlance over the cuisine, I thought," said one of them. "Enjoyed your disquisition on economics and things," said another, "I think we must do this again, don't you agree?" I did indeed.

Then it was off to bed with the lot and during the confusion and pother of this process I should tell you that I heard any number of unnerving yells. Though not given at the top of one's lungs, of course, I thought them each suitably astonishing in its own compact way.

By the time the children's bedtime was successfully accomplished Mrs. Baggs had a pot of chamomile tea waiting in the kitchen. She and Mr. Baggs and I sat to it and talked about proper literature for children and one thing and another. We played gin. I was able to manage two knocks, and Mr. Baggs four. Mrs. Baggs settled for a knock or two, herself, early on, but then, finding her stride, got several gins in a row and won the game going away, stifling yawns the while. She then excused herself and went to bed, apparently having some things she must do the next morning.

Opportune Baggs looked after her for a moment, then rose and fetched a bottle of blackberry port from the sideboard, decanted two glasses and raising one, solemnly said, "To that good wife."

"Hear, hear," I answered.

Baggs motioned for me to follow him. We went and stood listening for a moment at each of the children's bedrooms. From the truckle beds in those rooms came the most complex rhythms of small adenoidal mouse breathings it has ever been my privilege to hear. But nothing else. Satisfied, my host looked at me, his eyes dancing, and said, "Very well then. Shall we have a look at those drawings?"

We each carried a glass and a candle to his studio. He lit the hanging lantern there and pulled the drawings of an amazing invention, spreading them before me one by one, each from its own labeled cubbyhole in the wall. Setting a roll down and weighting one edge with his candlestick, he would, with an unselfconscious flourish of a paw, send the rest of it flying to the other end of the table where it would overshoot the edge to bounce in a graceful, springy curl partway to the floor. The effect was not unlike the opening of the curtain at a theatrical.

The first drawing was a plan view of the whole. I was overwhelmed with a bewildering complexity of lines and arrows and explanatory comments pointing to and elucidating several intricately drawn mechanisms. I saw things labeled "nib impellers" and "parchment straighteners" and "ink canals." I saw claw pull-downs and double claw pull-downs. There were toe excluders and elbow sockets, knee-crossovers and ankle extenders, a head bracket, ear standoffs—the scope of the thing was truly breathtaking.

He next pulled detailed drawings of the swoop-extenuators—a whole series of these ("The heart of the invention," he said quietly)—not only a top-to-bottom swoop-extenuator and left-to-right swoop-extenuator but also a top left of center to right very near the bottom swoop-extenuator and a diagonally inclining bottom leftward to upper right about a fourth of the way down swoop-extenuator and quite a few more.

Roll after roll received its due comment and explication from the inventor. Quiet, glowing and full of special information he was: "This is to be mortised, here, you see"; and "The ones in red are slipknots"; and "That is the underside you're looking at—magnified a bit"; and "Reverse thread there, of course. Wouldn't work at all, otherwise." I would nod, or frown gravely, or say something like "Hmm. Yes" to each explanation.

I came to learn that the hallmark of Opportune Baggs' inventions was adjustment. Everything about them positively bristled with thumbnuts and wingscrews and slip joints and tie-downs and notches numbered 1 2 3 4 and so forth. "Adjustment is the key," he said, simply. "I could do almost anything with this machine if I wanted to take the time to make the necessary adjustments. I could make butter with it. Easily! Shall I show you how?"

In the end he didn't. Rather, he sat and demonstrated the kinds of movements which the operator would make to use the invention for its intended purpose. Perched on the front edge of a chair, he rocked back and forth in one rhythm, right to left in another, slower, cycle—all the while moving his four limbs in various combinations of syncopated arcs and oscillations and humming quietly to imitate, I think, the overall effect of the various mechanisms moving in harmonious conjunction.

At length he stopped, suddenly, and slumped back into the chair, as if utterly spent by an excess of inventive zeal. Then, as suddenly, he rose and held his glass high over the drawings. The blackberry port smoldered like a darkling ruby in the lantern's light. I raised my glass, too.

"To mechanical calligraphy, then," he said.

"Mechanical calligraphy," I answered.

We stood for a long time in silence, both of us, I believe, trying to imagine what those wonderful flourishes and curlicues would look like—made with real ink on real parchment by a real Mousewriter.

CHAPTER 6

About Merchanty Swift Who Brought The Cheese Trade Down To Earth Almost Single-Handedly

It was normal to say of Merchanty Swift that he brought the cheese trade down to earth almost single-handedly. If you have not often been in the company of field mice you may, perhaps, need to be advised of the importance and nature of this sort of epigraphic extension which attaches itself to field mouse names. If a field mouse says something about Warburton Nines, for example, he will almost certainly say, in his opening reference, something like "... and then in came Warburton Nines Who Once Lifted A Cat." He will sometimes give you the complete epigraph—if he's feeling up to it and there's plenty of time—which would be "and then in came Warburton Nines, A Quite Large And Strong Mouse Who Once Lifted A Small Cat Clean Off The Ground And Has One Good Eye Left." But not to give either version when Warburton Nines came up in the conversation would be perceived as a slight discourtesy, at best, and in extreme cases outright shabbiness. Moreover, I would have you know that this kind of respect—it is called a *meritorious* epigraph—is not at all a hollow formality. Far from it. It is only given where it has been earned, and that soundly. Relatively few get it at every opening reference to their name, and, in fact, the higher the respect for the mouse the oftener the reference. A meritorious epigraph is a way of letting a mouse's deeds follow him. Quite nice, actually. But there are other kinds.

Some epigraphs adhere, not because of merit but for some other reason—interest, usually. I must pause here to say, right away, that there are NO negative epigraphs. Field mice would never have a thing like that. They are very forgiving, these mice, and hate gossip. They quite insist on fresh starts being given to whoever wants one. But they *are* fond of knowing interesting and distinctive things about one another. Or about anyone. They sometimes refer to me, for example, as "Waterford Hopstep Who Is Actually a Bird." As you can see, the epigraph has nothing to do with any merit of mine, but rather with an interesting accident of my lineage which I shall not take time to detail here. These are usually referred to as *distinguishing* epigraphs. "Opportune Baggs The Inventor" would be a kind of distinguishing epigraph. That is to say, it distinguishes him from most other mice, though it is not considered, particularly, a badge of honor or merit, as a meritorious epigraph would be. Though not of dishonor either, of course. Certainly not!

But to return to meritorious epigraphs for a moment: it must be said that sometimes they tend to grow. In the case of Merchanty Swift's, however, I am in an excellent position to credit it to the full. In any event, he almost always got the reference. But, as is so often the case, he hardly needed it, especially among the marriageable girls of the company. They were absolutely sick over him. He was very handsome, very dashing, he had been practically everywhere, and if he wasn't rich he could have been the moment he decided to stop giving whatever thing away to whoever asked him for it.

As to love, it was said that Pleasings Tatterstraw had broken Merchanty Swift's heart when she ran away with Henri de Rochefoot (a French mouse, I believe). There were, to be sure, many of those Tatterstraw girls but if one mentioned that fact to Merchanty Swift he would always say something like "Still, they're not Pleasings, are they?" and say it so dismissively and carelessly that that would be the end of it. After his heart was broken, then, he simply wasn't, as the Tottensea maidens put it, "interested." And, as refusal to sell is incentive to buy, the market raged.

But if something of a tragic figure in amours, Merchanty Swift was legendary in commerce and had certain accomplishments of exchange which were repeated by others in tones almost hushed for very awe. Preeminent among these, to be sure, was the cheese thing. It requires a small book, I'm afraid, to tell it, but if one is interested the account is available in any reputable mousebook shop. *Swift and Modern Cheeses* may sound a dry tome but in fact I've always thought it moves rather well, if one may be forgiven for saying so oneself, and it *is* populated by the most colorful characters of every stripe, from the darkest brigands of mongery—smugglers and hoarders and monopolists and the like—to the fairest heroes and heroines of the mercantile arts. One might enjoy it.

He appeared to all, Merchanty Swift, a casual fellow—easily met and full of good stories. But his coworkers and a few close friends knew him to be, in fact, almost meticulous. Indeed, though I am certain that there were times when he actually worried, he had such an enormous natural talent for what he did that his work appeared easy and effortless. It wasn't, of course. It was difficult, rigorous, often tedious, and occasionally dangerous. But there was this: he had nerves of steel, Merchanty Swift. Those who had seen him in the marketplace, toe to toe with bullies and wheedlers and flatterers and whiners—the whole panoply, in fact, of conscienceless higglers in the world—were certain that Merchanty Swift would come down in his price (or up his offer, as the case might be) exactly one mousesecond before his opponent (if buying) would huff away from the table having taken irremediable umbrage or (if selling) would hurl his wares back into his valise in an ostentatious gesture of undisguised finality. Those who witnessed such bargaining events were often heard to use the word "breathtaking" in their descriptions.

Whenever you called on Merchanty Swift, Mrs. Clementine Nickelpenny, his housekeeper, would serve you a very nice tea, but you were not likely to sit on the same chair twice. The one you sat on during your previous visit would have been traded for something better. Or for two somethings slightly worse. One of those, then, would have been bunched with four other articles which a linnet would have thought quite useless to begin with and sold at a handsome profit, which Merchanty Swift, often as not, would have placed in an unmarked envelope and slipped under the door of the Tottensea Foundling Home on his way to supper. Merchanty Swift cared nothing about things, you see. What really interested him was trading two of those things which he cared nothing about for another much better thing (which he cared nothing about either) and then showing it to you and asking you if you wanted it because he needed the room to put yet another thing which he had just acquired in trade a few moments ago—unless, of course, you wanted it, instead—in which case he wouldn't need the extra room anyway and, come to think of it, that would be an excellent solution to the problem!

In consequence of all this, Mrs. Nickelpenny had interesting experiences. One thinks, right away, of the storage crisis which ensued from the arrival, in midwinter, of no less than eighty-four mousepuncheons of pickled smolt when even the vast warehouses of Swift Mercantile Ltd. were already quite bulging with Scottish plaid, Irish linen, vanilla extract and a list of other things so long that it would require the remainder of this chapter, I suppose, to write it down. Issuing from that circumstance, all sleeping, dressing, bathing, visiting, reading of mail and other forms of general existence—to say nothing of eating and drinking!—had to take place in the Swift kitchen and rather in Mrs. Nickelpenny's way for several days running until the smolt, the linen and the extract could all find their way to proper markets.

Some of Mrs. Nickelpenny's interesting experiences had to do with a group of amiable bachelors who gathered once a month for dinner and cards at the home of Merchanty Swift. For those occasions, Mrs. Nickelpenny recruited her friend Mrs. Proserpine Pockets to help with the meals. And at one such event, while serving the meal in the dining room, Mrs. Nickelpenny and Mrs. Pockets overheard that this monthly gathering of more or less eligible associates had begun to refer to itself as The Unable to Find Wives Club. Upon their return to the kitchen, Mrs. Nickelpenny, who was a widow and felt quite eligible, herself, as it happened, said to Mrs. Pockets, also a widow, "Did you hear that, dearie? The Unable to Find Wives Club indeed! I put it to you, Proserpine Pockets: am I invisible? Are you?" And, with that, Mrs. Nickelpenny committed two muffin pans to the kitchen sink rather more noisily than might have been required.

Mrs. Pockets only smiled but Mrs. Nickelpenny, somewhat overflowing with the very idea, said, "All right, then. They'll not find us calling it The Unable to Find Wives Club. You and I, my dear, shall call it The Not Paying Attention Club." And so they did. And, as I think their complaint reasonable and just, so shall I.

CHAPTER 7

The Not Paying Attention Club

The Not Paying Attention Club, though a bit fluid in its membership, usually consisted of Merchanty Swift, the host, Peebles Carryforth The Mayor, Sir Rotherham Twickets, Umpteen Weeks, who was pretty old and knew things, Leacock Hardesty The Younger (of Hardesty & Hardesty), General Random Chewings and Warburton Nines Who Once Lifted A Cat. And these might be joined for dinner by a fine little fellow named Farnaby Pockets, who, though he sometimes helped his mother with the serving, was more often to be found sitting at the table as Merchanty Swift's special guest.

On one occasion, an hour before the club was to arrive, Mr. Swift informed Mrs. Nickelpenny, with emphatic apologies, that the china and crystal which had been laid on the dining room table since half a day previous must be taken up at once as they had unfortunately been included in a recent transaction involving certain commodities. He was happy to add, however, that a fine set of stoneware and some pewter tankards, which should serve very nicely for the evening's purpose, would be arriving within the hour along with sixteen quires of writing paper, twelve mousebolts of houndstooth, three gills of quite good treacle and eighteen and a half cases of reasonably good scuppernong (which could hardly be got anywhere in those days, he said. At any price).

In point of actual fact, an unfortunate delay in the delivery of these items resulted in the dinner being served somewhat later than originally planned. Mrs. Nickelpenny, therefore, was forced to report to her employer that there was a slight inconvenience involving the material absence of certain eating and drinking apparatus which would be more or less required were the meal to go forward.

Merchanty Swift, ever given to quick thinking, turned immediately to General Random Chewings, who proved more than equal to the occasion by passing a wonderfully diverting half hour with a military lesson for the layman on the art of turning an enemy's flank—a spirited presentation liberally sprinkled with quotations from von Clausewitz and illustrated across Mrs. Nickelpenny's almost empty tablecloth in such a way that the saltcellar and the pepper caster, though quite surprised by a predawn attack from the napkin rings and taking heavy losses in the early going, were able, ultimately, to marshal the forks in countermeasure, and, keeping the spoons in reserve until the cream jug had been irretrievably committed, carried the day in an absolute rout. "Ha!" cried the General, triumphantly, at the final dispositions, as he struck the table in a slight overplus of martial excitement. "Ha!" cried Farnaby Pockets, as well (without intending to, I think).

Peebles Carryforth The Mayor was greatly entertained and

instructed, along with the others, but in him there were misgivings. A very solid mouse was Peebles Carryforth: deliberate, circumspect, a bit serious at times, perhaps, but quite well-liked and, I think, on the whole, a handsome mouse, though some said his whiskers were tragically short and all agreed that he could have lost a bit of weight. But he was, after all, a bachelor, wasn't he? He was a good mayor, a humble leader who stayed mostly behind the scenes, guiding by example and persuasion and gathering what wisdom he might at the lonely pinnacles of mouse leadership. And on this evening, the Mayor was disquieted. Something was not right, he thought.

General Random Chewings was not, of course, a real general—not a military general, I mean. He always wanted to be one, it's true, and he had studied the arts of war since childhood. It was, in fact, a matter of the deepest disappointment to him that he could *not* be a general, and he had frankly wondered, in this connection, if, perhaps, there had been some mistake in his origins. He was much loved by the mice of Tottensea and greatly valued for his recondite knowledge. It was a mysterious thing to them, war. They knew nothing about it and, accordingly, they regarded it—and him—with a kind of awe. They made him General of Tottensea Burrows, having not the slightest idea what that would be, and gave him a uniform.

It was a handsome uniform—dignified and conservative. The mice all nodded and said "Very practical" to one another when they saw the tunic and felt it. It was Prussian blue with a high standing collar and button loops the color of toast. "Just the thing," they thought. The hat was a bicorne—

jet-black with some plumes on it. Merchanty Swift found the outfit somewhere in his travels, brought it back and had it altered. The mice then presented it to Random Chewings at a brisk little ceremony one Saturday morning in the early spring. There were short speeches and things to eat. Every mouse there smiled broadly at other mice and was pleased. They do love that sort of thing.

The General of Tottensea Burrows was not a real general for the simple and very excellent reason that there is no such thing as an army of field mice. There couldn't be! It's simply not in them. They have courage, yes. Some of them have a great deal of courage. But they could hardly be persuaded to harm anyone, you see. No, no. They are not warriors. They are nerved and sinewed for the other things: for escape and hiddenness. It is their glory to disappear—to be quick and to vanish, to melt right into the briar and sedge. Theirs it is to baffle and confuse the predator's eye, to astonish with sheer evanescence—seen threading through stalk and stem, and abruptly gone! A vapor! Suddenly down into the deep fortress of the earth they would be, racing through the clever tunnels, through straits too narrow and turns too sharp for the enemies who hungered after them and wanted them.

All this, of course, Peebles Carryforth knew, had known for a very long time. But it was at this particular meeting of The Not Paying Attention Club that he saw—and saw clearly—what was not right about Tottensea Burrows. It was at this meeting that he saw that Tottensea Burrows was, in fact, misplaced. But he was a leader, Peebles Carryforth, and it was part of his wisdom to know when his mice were ready to face facts and when they weren't. So he kept his own counsel for the moment and awaited his opportunity.

After the dining table had been reclaimed from the noise and fume of war and had been returned to more gentle purposes, Mrs. Nickelpenny and Mrs. Pockets served a superb carrot loaf, garnished with a parsley wreath and accompanied by stuffed marrow and various trimmings—all nicely truffled and beautifully set out on whatever silver tray Merchanty Swift happened to own that week. It was greatly enjoyed and remarked upon, that meal—and eaten, too, off stoneware plates which had, at length, arrived and which everyone, to the last guest, thought handsome in the extreme and as well worth waiting for as any plates they had ever been slightly inconvenienced by—which inconvenience, they went on to emphasize, was so minimal as to be hardly worth mentioning in any event.

And they were greatly taken with the tankards. Absolutely loved the tankards! All pewter and weighty they were— rather masculine, in their opinions—with hinged lids which might be counted on, they thought, to keep a mouse's ale from going flat while he went on with his eating. Exactly right for their purposes and all of them pleaded with great passion for Merchanty Swift to *please* keep these tankards and not trade them away next week for venetian blinds or enameled toothpicks or some awful thing! And when Swift saw their depth of feeling he was moved to promise that these tankards would never go onto the block! No, not in the fiercest

heat of commercial exchange, he said, would he be tempted to throw *these* tankards into the clinch of some difficult bargain. These tankards would be for his friends.

They all said hurrah to that and, knowing their mouse, never did they worry. For though they knew him to be rather devoted to a bit of trading, they knew him to be even more devoted to his friends.

During the eating, just after the General had asked the group whether anyone in the world could make a vegetable aspic as well as Clementine Nickelpenny, Merchanty Swift turned to Master Pockets, who sat just to his right, and said, "How does it go with rocks these days, Farnaby Pockets?"

"Very well, thank you, sir," the young mouse replied.

"Any good ones, recently?"

"Oh, yes sir! I found a very nice one in the rockery. It looks ever so much like a frog on the one side of it."

"Ah, capital," said Sir Rotherham, taking up the subject. "And on the other side, then?"

"Hmm," Farnaby pondered. "On the other side it looks more like a rock, sir."

"Yes, well," consoled Sir Rotherham. "To be expected I suppose. Still, in all, very nice on the one side?"

"Yes sir," said Farnaby Pockets.

"And how are you mending, by the way?" Merchanty Swift asked his young guest.

"I'm quite recovered, sir."

"Ah. That's good hearing, Farnaby. You gave us a start, you know."

"Have you been ill, then?" asked the Mayor.

"Oh, no sir," Farnaby said. "Not ill, exactly. It's just that . . . I jumped, sir."

"You jumped?" the Mayor said, uncertain.

"Yes sir. Off something."

"I see," said the Mayor, cautiously. "Are you given to jumping?"

"Not so as I used to be, sir."

"And was there an umbrella involved, perhaps, *in* the jumping?" the Mayor wanted to know.

"Yes sir, there was."

"Hmm. Ineffective was it—the brolly?"

"Yes sir."

"Came right down, did you?"

"Like a stone, sir."

"Yes, well," the Mayor said, and clucked his tongue, gravely.

"Shockingly bad parachutes, brollies!" Sir Rotherham said, making a face. "Still, lesson learned and all that, I suppose."

"Yes sir," Farnaby said.

"We must all learn to measure our risks," the Mayor put in, looking around at the others rather pointedly.

"And to check with one's mother before doing some things. Hmm?" said Merchanty Swift, cheerfully, looking at Farnaby from under raised eyebrows.

"Yes sir."

"Were you badly injured, then, Pockets?" Sir Rotherham asked.

"I broke my leg, sir!"

"I daresay!" Sir Rotherham exclaimed. "Was there anyone to help you?"

"No sir. Not at first, there wasn't. But then Mr. Pickerel happened by."

"Pickerel, you say? Would that be *Langston* Pickerel?" Sir Rotherham asked, somehow surprised at the thought.

"Yes sir. And he carried me right home to me mum!"

"Did he indeed?" Sir Rotherham exclaimed. "Langston Pickerel happened by and carried you to your mum. Well now, *there's* a thing!"

"It certainly is," said Merchanty Swift.

"Langston Pickerel." Sir Rotherham mused to himself, still in some amazement.

"He's quite a colorful chap, Pickerel," Merchanty Swift said. "Has his own ideas about things."

"I daresay!" Sir Rotherham replied to that.

"And I think we must give him every credit for his kindness to young Pockets, here," Swift went on.

"Hear, hear," Sir Rotherham said, governing his tongue, decently, and passing on without gossip. Langston Pickerel was, after all, the most tempting subject in all of Tottensea Burrows for gossip. I would go further to say that sometimes, in fact, only the most stringent discipline was sufficient to produce the necessary forbearance to avoid gossip where Langston Pickerel was concerned!

"Tell me, Swift," the Mayor said, changing the subject, "in your travels, you must see lots of field mouse communities."

"To be sure," said the host.

"And do you find Tottensea Burrows to be . . . umm . . . typical in its situation."

"Certainly not," answered Merchanty Swift. "I'll thank you for another of those truffles, Hardesty."

"How's that, Swift? Not typical, you say?" asked Sir Rotherham, disturbed at the very thought of his community being irregular in some way.

"No, actually, not typical at all, placed hard by The Cottage, here, as we are."

"Oh, that," Sir Rotherham said. "Well, that's rather an advantage, isn't it? Convenient foraging and all."

"It'll be the ruin of us!" said a brusque voice near the end of the table. They all turned to look at Umpteen Weeks.

"Do you think so?" asked the Mayor.

"We don't know flippin' nothin' 'bout bein' field mice these days," said Umpteen Weeks. "Gone all soft, we have ... eatin' after birds and a dog of all things! When I was a nipper we lived in the fields like *proper* field mice. Had everything mice could want, we did. Pretty safe it was, too. Knew our way around the hedgerows like the backs of our paws. Didn't live underfoot of no man and no woman. I can tell you that!"

"So you didn't," said the Mayor. "How did you come here, then?"

"I was brought, wasn't I? By my family."

"Ever think of going *back* to the fields, Weeks?"

"And leave my relations?"

"Hmm, I see," said the Mayor. "No, of course not."

And just at that moment, to the great satisfaction of everyone at table, Clementine Nickelpenny and Proserpine Pockets brought in the trifle.

CHAPTER 8

Poker and Cheroots

After dinner, in the drawing room, there was card playing.
With Mrs. Pockets and Farnaby gone home and Mrs. Nickelpenny well retired to her rooms, members of the club
thought it meet to indulge themselves in games of skill and
chance. They normally began with a riotous thing called
Mole Biscuits.

I've never played Mole Biscuits, myself, though I have
watched it being played—for all the good it did me. I find it
fairly impossible, actually. On this evening, I am told, General Random Chewings innocently put forth a card only to be
suddenly and gleefully advised by Mayor Peebles Carryforth that one may *not* play a black six while the red knaves
are on the board. "Honestly, Chewings!" the Mayor said,
laughing hugely. "What were you thinking!" The General,
then, having struck his forehead in self-reproach and saying
"Crumbs! How could I have forgot that!" was required to
exchange places with Umpteen Weeks at the foot of the
table, and did so in jovial humiliation to the extreme merriment of all other players.

A moment later, Sir Rotherham's card no sooner left his

paw than Leacock Hardesty erupted with "Aha! You can't DO that!" and went on about the utter impropriety of forfeiting a nine of any color while a black ten resides in the queue! "Pay up! Pay up!" the others shouted immediately and Sir Rotherham had then to give tokens to Warburton Nines, who was acting banker at the moment, and replace General Chewings at the foot. The General, then, advancing *from* the foot, was entitled to challenge Merchanty Swift for dealership and beat him badly with a throw of dice. "He's out! He's out!" came the cry. And on it went like that. It's entirely uproarious, Mole Biscuits, and seems always to end in exhausting and somewhat breathless hilarity.

Having recovered from Mole Biscuits, then, the membership was fortified with strong black coffee and cinnamon cheroots (which, unlike tobacco cheroots, by the way, are *not* to be set on fire in order to be enjoyed!) and the evening concluded with a somewhat fierce competition at poker.

Merchanty Swift, he of the steel nerves who can sell practically anything, was something of a legend at poker as well as at commerce. His primary competition within the club came from Warburton Nines, who was certainly formidable, but who, to be fair, had the unquestioned advantage of hardly ever saying anything to anyone about anything! Indeed, no one ever had the slightest idea *what* the Nines was thinking, let alone what cards he might be holding. And if that were not enough, he had an eye patch, didn't he?

They played five-card draw with the dealer laying out, there being only enough cards in the pack for six players. The Mayor dealt first and as the opening bets were trickling in, he said, as casually as possible, "I do wonder about our situation at times."

"Situation?" Sir Rotherham asked.

"Tottensea Burrows. Here. So close to The Cottage."

"Oh. That again."

"Well, we have no natural protections here, you see."

"Protections? From what?"

"From whatever," said the Mayor. "And if we were driven out, say . . . would we know how to provide for ourselves out there? Cards?"

"Driven out?" said General Random Chewings. "Smoke and spinach! That'd take a bit of starting over, now, wouldn't it? Two cards, please."

"How should we be driven out?" Sir Rotherham asked with some indignation. "Two as well."

"Three cards, please," Merchanty Swift said. "It only requires a cat, Sir Rotherham."

"I daresay!"

Umpteen Weeks took two cards, Hardesty one, and Warburton Nines stood pat.

"Yes, one cat," Swift said. "You can ask my housekeeper about that. Are you betting, General?"

"Tuppence," Random Chewings said, tossing his bet into the pot.

Sir Rotherham folded.

"Hmm, that was brisk," Swift said and put in coins of his own. "Two and two more."

Weeks and Hardesty matched the bet. Warburton Nines said, "Your pence, my shilling," and that was the end of that.

As the General shuffled the pack, Sir Rotherham asked, "What's this about your housekeeper, Swift?"

"Mrs. Nickelpenny lost her whole family to a cat, you know," Swift said.

"I daresay!"

"Mrs. Pockets did, as well—except for one little one. That would be Farnaby, of course."

"How really terrible it must have been for them!" the General said compassionately. He stopped dealing and looked up.

"Terrible it was, General," Swift said, sadly. "I came across them quite by accident—running for their lives from Flitch's Farm. It was ghastly—Mrs. Nickelpenny, mauled and bleeding, Mrs. Pockets, hurt as well and with a babe-in-arms at that."

"I didn't know they came from Flitch's," Leacock Hardesty said with mild surprise.

"Yes, indeed," Swift answered. "Sweetcream Burrows. Handsome place. Right up against the milking parlor at Flitch's, it was."

"Bit like us, then," the Mayor said. "Close on to humans, I mean."

"Yes," Swift said. "Too close, in their case, as it turned out. Very posh while it lasted, though—'peaches and cream' if ever there was. But then old Flitch took a turn, it seems. Fed up with field mice, I suppose. Put in a grimalkin from the town and it was all up with Sweetcream Burrows. Fierce old cat, she was. Took them in twos and threes, they said! A massacre beyond the telling—Nickelpenny and the two Pockets barely getting out with their lives."

The General resumed his dealing. "So you brought the poor things here and took them in."

"Yes. Though I only had employment for one of them, in the end. But Mrs. Pockets is very resourceful and thought she might have a go at fixing up the old inn."

"And so she did," the Mayor said.

"And did it beautifully, too," agreed the General. "We're all very proud of her. Bets, please."

"Thruppence," Sir Rotherham said grandly, rather pleased with himself. Terrible at poker, Sir Rotherham.

The final event of the evening was referred to as The Foundlings' Cut. It was seven-card stud, a game they picked up one night at The Silver Claw from a desert mouse who claimed to be in from Nevada. They had mixed feelings about the mouse, actually, but they liked his game and included it in their monthly routine. They set it up to require large and increasing minimum bets after each round. The pot, accordingly, grew often to ridiculous proportions, absorbing practically all the evening's winnings and sometimes a bit more than that. At the end, as you might guess, the money was set apart to be sent over to the foundlings on the following morning.

It was a nerve-racking affair, The Foundlings' Cut, and the cheroots were sometimes gnawed to mutilation by the time it was over. Warburton Nines, who was dealing, turned up two red aces quickly and Umpteen Weeks looked good, right through, for an eight-high straight. The Mayor had a pair of threes and the General even less. Sir Rotherham showed early promise but faded in the heat. Swift came to the front with three tens showing (two blacks and a diamond), betting two shillings six, which sent Mayor and General alike out of the hand by the fifth card. Hardesty stayed with a possible flush but he fidgeted badly and lacked authority.

The drama turned on the sixth card. Warburton Nines, icy and methodical, turned up a third ace! Spades. Umpteen Weeks looked severe and Leacock Hardesty unaccountably bit right through his cheroot. Swift hardly noticed, one might have thought, watching as he was for a fourth ten. But it was a six of clubs.

"Half a sovereign," Warburton Nines announced importantly. Swift shrugged and paid. Hardesty looked anxious and quit. Weeks made vague noises and dropped out, as well.

Nines dealt the last card—down—and looked at it. "Twelve shillings," he said, stacking the coins carefully and pushing them to the center of the table.

Swift looked at his card. "Raise you a quid!" he said brightly and with a hint of mischief.

Lightning from a clear sky, that was, to the dealer. And it showed on his face. But he got up the sovereign and more. "Add a guinea," he growled, throwing it in with as near a flourish as anyone had ever seen from Warburton Nines.

On they went—Nines and Swift—up and up. Witnesses disagree on the number of raises, but it was Swift who ended it.

"Let's have a look, then," he said, simply, and the room was certain they had finally seen to the very bottom of the Merchanty Swift nerves of steel.

When the look came, the onlookers gasped audibly. Warburton Nines *did,* in fact, absolutely, have the aces—all of them! They looked at one another, wondering. Did Swift have the fourth ten? Would he go quietly without turning over his cards? No indeed! He would show. And more than that, turning up the seven/eight/nine of clubs to go with his six/ten, he would win. Home and dry.

The room burst into a strange, spontaneous applause. No one knew why. Perhaps it was joy for the foundlings. The pot was, after all, as rich as anyone could remember. Yes. It was very good for the foundlings, that game. But it didn't do the Merchanty Swift legend any harm, either.

CHAPTER 9

Something About Me

or

An Early Mistake in Life and What Came of It

At some point in this account, I suppose, I must pause to say one or two things about myself. One does not wish to put oneself forward unbecomingly, but as you might question what the deuce I'm doing in this story to begin with, I think it only fair to say something by way of explanation. (Readers do have *some* rights, in my opinion.) And whatever I may have led you blithely to believe, linnets are not, after all, in the habit of consorting with field mice.

One may sometimes wonder at events. What if, for example, in one's childhood a certain lack of orientation led one to an unfortunate act? If one misstepped, say, when very young, not at all thinking to be reckless, could one, nevertheless, be thought of as "getting what was coming to him," as they say? Or might it have been a happy occurrence, after all—this misstepping? Might awful things sometimes provide the setting, so to speak, for things wonderful? So there's a question, isn't it?

I fell out of the nest. Now, it's no good asking *linnets* about the meaning of a thing like that. Nothing against linnets. I am in a position to say that they are quite wonderful in their own way. It's just that there are certain things you ask linnets and certain things you might just as well *not* ask linnets. It's difficult to explain. Here:

A linnet knows the proper thing to do. If you were to suggest to a linnet that perhaps he should do something in a new or different way the linnet would look at you in such a fashion as to make you wonder if he even heard what you said. And if he did hear you, and even if you could be sure that he understood you in some way, he wouldn't have the slightest idea how to push on to thinking about what you had just suggested.

I, myself, learned to think about things from the mice. An early experience in this education came when one of them asked my opinion about something. Linnets never ask you that. They do not have opinions. They know a thing or they don't. One may know the proper diet for nestlings or one may not. But there are no opinions about it. They don't *think* about things, you see, they *know* about things. They are hardworking and successful and very likable, in my view, but they would never ask you what you think. It wouldn't occur to them.

The mice, on the other hand, are unendingly curious about what you think. And they often ask you in just that way. "Well, what do you think?"

To an unsuspecting linnet, such a question would be unnerving. Why would you want to know what was happening inside his brain? You might just as well ask him what was happening inside his gizzard. He wouldn't have the slightest idea about that either, and he would wonder, uneasily, why you cared.

You could inquire about the correct way to build a nest and the linnet would give you an excellent account. Or "Where should one look out for stone flies or onion thrips?" would be quite a comfortable question for him. He would be on home ground there, you see, and I don't doubt he would give you an extensive and well-organized reply. In fact, he would very likely offer to show you, in a practical way, how to go about finding stone flies and onion thrips and any number of other things if you were interested *and* if he could spare the time. They are wonderfully helpful, linnets, but they do keep awfully busy.

When I was first asked by a field mouse what I thought about something, I stood, beak agape, and pondered the concept. Then, after a space, the question began to please me. I felt important for some reason.

"You must have an opinion," the mouse said to me, waiting.

I remember wondering if perhaps he was right. And if he *was* right, what must it be like? To have one, I mean. An opinion. In the end, I blurted out something. As an opinion, it wouldn't have amounted to very much, I think, but I was surpassingly proud of having had it and, moreover, I'm certain to have gone on about it at some length. It was thrilling!

I wouldn't have you think that linnets don't wish to talk. On the contrary, they very much enjoy talking. It's just that they don't talk about ideas, or about the meaning of things, you see. They talk about . . . things that have *happened* to them—or to someone they know. Incidents, in fact, are extremely interesting to them. If he took a green lacewing in midair, for example, or if she had some unpleasantness with a meadow pipit over a bit of nesting material, a linnet would tell you about it in fine detail. So you might overhear any one of them saying something like:

. . . It was brilliant. I saw the thing on an alder twig, you see. And, just as I spotted him and was on my way, he flew. Now, whether he knew I was after him or just happened to fly at that moment I haven't the faintest idea. I don't know a thing about lacewings, do you? Anyway, I lifted high into the clearing and got above him. And when I fell upon him—why, you would have thought me a swallow! . . .

or:

. . . Then I said to the pipit, "Not while I'm about, you won't!" And she said to me, in the rudest sort of way, "We'll see about that, then!" And so you can imagine how I felt, having gone all the way out there to *find* thistledown in the first place, and with all I've got to do these days I'll certainly have no patience with a meadow pipit who *lives* out there, for goodness' sake, and can have any *amount* of thistledown for the taking whenever she wants it! . . .

So, you see, it isn't that linnets don't talk. Dear me! Very much to the contrary. But I must get on. I was speaking of falling out of nests.

I surely made quite a spectacle of myself, flopping about on the ground (my poor overworked parents being away shopping for insects at the time). I somehow succeeded, without plan, to flop and hop myself right out from under the beech tree, across the lawn and into the wisteria climbers at the base of the chimney. There I was, then: frightened, shivering, eyes darting about—utterly devoid of any slightest notion what to do next. I can't think what should have become of me had it not been for a small "Hullo!" somewhere behind me.

I turned round. A mouseling of about my own age stood peeking round a vine root at me. He just watched me for a bit, his mouth hanging open with curiosity and his whiskers seriously busy at that little quivery thing they do.

"I'm Opportune Baggs," he said, finally.

I didn't say anything. I just stared at him.

"And you?" he asked.

I said not a peep.

"I'm a field mouse, as it happens," Opportune Baggs said.

I just stared. After quite a long time he said, "You might say *something*."

But I didn't. After another long silence he asked me if I wanted a biscuit. Receiving no answer, he disappeared down a hole which I hadn't noticed until he went into it. After a bit he returned with his mother. They both peered at me, their heads barely sticking up out of the hole.

"It's a baby linnet, I believe," Mrs. Baggs said. "He's very frightened, the poor thing." Then, to me, she said, "Can we help you, dear?" I shivered and stared. "Are you from the beech tree, then?" she asked.

"He won't say *anything*, Mother," Opportune said. "I've tried ever so hard to get him to, but he won't. Not a word."

"Is your nest in the climbers, dear?" Mrs. Baggs asked me. After waiting in vain for a reply, she said, "No. He isn't going to talk to us, is he?"

Just then I was startled by another voice from behind me. "What's this, then?" the voice said. I turned round to find a grown mouse almost upon me. I hopped away a little.

"It's a baby linnet, Papa!" Opportune said. "I found him. He's out of his nest."

"Yes. I can see that," said Mr. Baggs.

"He won't say *anything* to us," Opportune told him.

"No. He wouldn't, would he?" said Mr. Baggs, sounding very wise.

"But, why won't he?" Opportune asked.

"He's too frightened, isn't he?" Mr. Baggs said. "Besides, his mother may have told him not to, you see."

"Oh!" Opportune Baggs said, respectfully, placing a paw over his mouth. He hadn't thought of that.

"Look," Mr. Baggs said, changing the subject. "We must get inside. You'll have to keep the children in for a few days, I'm afraid, dear. There's a stoat about."

"A stoat! Where?" Mrs. Baggs asked, unsettled.

"Umpteen Weeks saw him this morning. In the bushes by the beech tree. He was cleaning out a linnet's nest, the stoat was."

Mrs. Baggs took in her breath sharply. They all looked at me. "Oh, the poor dear," she said.

"Yes. Pity," Mr. Baggs said. "Well, we'd better get inside, I suppose."

"But what about the linnet!" Opportune said, with alarm.

Mr. Baggs looked at me, then. He scratched his head. He walked toward me a little, stooped, awkwardly, and said, "Umm. Look, old chap. You really must stay out of sight for a bit. All right? And you won't be calling for your mum just now, will you? It's a bit risky, you see."

"Papa!" Opportune Baggs said, his alarm growing.

"Is there anything we can do, dear?" Mrs. Baggs asked Mr. Baggs.

He looked at her.

"Anything at *all,* do you think?" she said, with a very earnest look.

Mr. Baggs looked at me, then back at Mrs. Baggs. He said, "What? What could we do? Surely you don't mean . . ."

But, of course, she *did* mean. Exactly.

CHAPTER 10

The Flying Mouse

A field mouse burrow is a very odd place for a linnet to be. Mr. Baggs thought so, too, though he was very kind to me and made the best of it. I sat in the corner of the kitchen and watched them eat their supper. I heard things being said like "May I have the jam pot, please," and "Is there more tea, then?" and "Stop staring at him. Opportune was staring at the linnet, Mother," and "Lower your voice, Arabella. Opportune, don't stare," and "But he stares at us, Mother. That's all he does is stare," and "That will be quite enough, young mouse. You are not to talk back to your mother."

Mrs. Baggs was very concerned that I wouldn't eat and fussed over me, terribly, throughout the meal. I was, in fact, quite hungry, but not interested in anything they were eating and too shy to ask for something else. Failing to persuade me to join them at table she, several times, brought bits of food to me in the corner. I watched her but ate nothing. Finally, after trying several things, she looked at me and said, "You must be starving, dear. Isn't there *something* I can get you?"

I said, "I should like an insect, please."

Everyone at the table looked at me and their jaws dropped. It was the first thing I had said to them. Although mice will sometimes eat insects, in a pinch, these mice are quite cultured and would hardly think of doing it under any circumstances. The children, in fact, said, "Eew!" and stifled giggles, noisily, with their paws over their mouths. Mr. Baggs began to laugh and went on laughing as he got up, put on his cap and went out to get me some insects.

The next day, Opportune and Arabella Baggs took it upon themselves, to teach me to fly. As it had to be done indoors, on account of the stoat, the lesson took place in the sitting room. Opportune began by reading to me from an article about flying which he had found in the mouse encyclopedia.

"It all sounds simple enough," he said. "Here, listen to this:

> If the upper surface of a wing is curved while the lower surface is flat, the air is caused to move faster over the top than along the bottom. This causes the air pressure at the top to be less than at the bottom and produces something called lift."

He then looked at me, thoughtfully, and said, "Hmm. Let's see your wing, linnet."

"We can't call him 'linnet,'" Arabella said.

"Why not?" Opportune asked her. "What do you want to call him?"

"I want to call him by his name," she said.

"But we don't know that, do we?"

"Well, we're not calling him linnet. Ask him his name."

"I've already asked him that. He wouldn't tell us. He's very shy."

"Well, ask him again."

"You ask him," Opportune said. "As you seem to know everything about everything."

"No. He's your linnet. Ask him."

"All right," Opportune said, and sighed. "Look, friend. I'm Opportune Baggs, as I said. And this bossy thing, here, The Empress of All Living Mice, is my sister. Her name is Arabella. What's yours, then?"

After waiting for a bit Opportune said, "There. You see. He isn't going to tell us. Let's get on with the flying."

"Just a moment," Arabella said. "Don't rush him. These things take time, often as not."

We all waited. At last, getting up my nerve, I said, in a very small voice, "Waterford."

"There!" Arabella screeched, triumphantly. "Waterford. His name is Waterford!"

"Yes, I heard that," said Opportune, clearing his throat and going on hurriedly "Now, ahem . . . Waterford, we need to have a look at your wing. If you could just . . ."

"Mother!" Arabella shrieked at the top of her lungs. "I've found out his name!" And off she ran to the kitchen to tell about it. By the time she returned with Mrs. Baggs, Opportune had got me to extend a wing and was examining it.

"Your name is Waterford!" Mrs. Baggs said, coming in all smiles and encouragement. "How wonderful! It's a lovely name." Then she said to Opportune, "What are you doing, dear?"

"Having a look at his wing. Look at this, Mother. It's supposed to be flat on the bottom. Would you call that flat?"

"No, I wouldn't call it flat, exactly."

"Nor would I," Opportune said. "Could you try flattening it, Waterford?" he asked me.

"What makes you think it's supposed to be flat?" asked Mrs. Baggs.

"Look, here. There's a drawing."

"Oh, I don't believe so, darling. He's not an aeroplane, is he?"

And, at that, The Empress of All Living Mice collapsed onto the floor in an extravagant fit of hysterical laughter. Poor Opportune was quite humiliated, said to his sister, "All right, then. *You* teach him to fly!" and left the room, his dignity in shreds.

His mother went after him, saying. "No, darling. It was an honest mistake." She turned back to say, "Arabella, shame on you!"

I, for my part, was left in the sitting room—a shy young linnet, only partially fledged and with a small hysterical field mouse rolling about my feet on the floor. I folded my wing, sat very still and felt bad about everything.

That evening, after supper, in the sitting room, Mr. Baggs told us that a bird wing was not so different from an aeroplane wing, after all, and that it actually worked on the same principle. At this, Opportune Baggs made an alarmingly unpleasant face at his sister, Arabella Baggs, who was sitting across the room from him. Mr. Baggs then went on to say that birds were, however, quite different from aeroplanes in that they didn't have engines to pull them along, did they? When, at that, Arabella Baggs made an appallingly unpleasant face at her brother, Mrs. Baggs thought it would be best for Opportune and Arabella to turn and face their respective walls during the remainder of family time.

Mr. Baggs said that the most important thing about all this was that I was, after all, *a bird*. That, of course, made me very proud. He then said that, being one, I would fly exactly like a bird when the time came. At that, though still very proud, I must confess I was slightly anxious into the bargain. He seemed to understand this, for he looked directly at me and said, "It's *in* you, Waterford! Our part is to give you a home, protect you from your enemies and give you time to grow. But we shan't teach you how to fly. No, no. When your feathers are all in and your limbs strong, we shall take you outside, get you up onto something off the ground, and then, my dear Waterford, we shall all stand back while *you* teach *us* how a bird flies!"

It was almost like that. The time having come, they got me somehow onto the roof of the potting shed through the good services of a recumbent garden cart against its wall and a convenient forsythia bush planted next to it. The entire Baggs family then stood on the ground below me and looked up, squinting expectantly into the morning light. I perched on the edge of the slates and looked down.

Arabella said, "No, don't look down!"

"Shhh," Mr. Baggs whispered. "Let him be. He must get used to the idea, you see."

"Yes, let him be!" Opportune said, reinforcing the thought in a very loud and rasping whisper. "He must get used to the idea!"

So they all let me be. For a long time. For a *very* long time, I'm afraid.

Finally, the tension having reached unbearable levels, Mrs. Baggs, still looking up steadily and shading her eyes from the sun, said to me, in a calm and encouraging voice, "Do something with your wings, dear."

And I did. I flew—with no idea *how* I was doing it, in awful terror, losing altitude—and at the end of it somehow found myself on the grape arbor. The Baggses rushed over and sent up rousing cheers and congratulations from below while I clung desperately to the lattice, crazed with mindless exhilaration, panting wildly and grinning without stint. My heart races to think of it!

It was a happy time, my sojourn with the Baggs family. At length, I got past my shyness and went on to feel quite at home with them—and with all the mice of Tottensea Burrows, in fact. I ate their foods. I had opinions. I talked of ideas. And as things went on, though very much a linnet, I became so free in the company of field mice and so abreast of their ways that I am, to this day, often referred to in these environs as the flying mouse.

CHAPTER 11

Unwanted Attentions

Tottensea Burrows was, generally speaking, a quite literate community. While saying nothing against that, I think I should point out that the appeal of The Bookish Mouse to a young male of the Burrows might have had little or nothing to do with the actual reading of books. It might, on the other hand, have had much or everything to do with three beautiful Fieldpea girls who would help him find the very mousebook he was looking for, whether or not he had the slightest intention of reading it!

And it might be that said young male would be inquired of—by a friend or, indeed, even by his mother!—about unusually frequent visits to the bookshop.

"Have you finished with that book, already?" he might be asked. "You only just bought it."

"Yes, I know, Mother," he might say in reply, "but it was very poorly written, wasn't it? And my interest began to flag, I'm afraid, about a third of the way in." Or, if it was a nonfiction book, he might say that he had decided to look into related books which could be read along with it to give a mouse a sense of balance and proportion and to prevent his being unduly influenced by a single author.

In summary, suffice it to say that Grenadine, Almandine and Incarnadine Fieldpea were much sought after. One or the other of them was often chosen "queen" of these or those games, or "princess" of this or that fair, and they attracted many suitors—not all of which they wanted. Grenadine had, for example, at one point, a most distressing and unwanted suit pressed upon her by an unusual personage who went by the name of Mr. Langston Pickerel.

There was, I think, no more remarkable sight in all of Tottensea Burrows than Langston Pickerel dressed up. Should he wish to impress, he had but to appear in, say, his Italian blue doublet with the military braid, worn over a waistcoat of crimson, probably, and overslung with a woolen sash filled absolutely to the full with badges and medals and other such brightware—all of this to be girded at the waist by a silver buckled patent leather strap from which would hang, in most cases, his splendid Saracen dagger with the three tourmalines worked cleverly among the carbuncles along the hilt. At such times, I'm afraid, he was utterly rakish without competition. And he knew it.

On an afternoon, there appeared at the Fieldpea door a mole, dressed quite to the nines in black livery and holding, in one paw, a modest but courtly bouquet of heliotrope and, in the other, a small silver tray—a salver, as it's sometimes called—on the surface of which rested a white envelope addressed to Miss Grenadine Fieldpea. The envelope was sealed with a dollop of wax which was stamped with an ornamented figure of some type which they finally decided was the letter "P," but it was adorned with so many scrolly lines and what-have-yous that it was impossible to be certain.

"For Miss Grenadine Fieldpea," the mole said, stiffly, without looking at Mr. Fieldpea.

"Thank you. I'll see that she gets them," Mr. Fieldpea said.

"An answer is requested," the mole said, solemnly, keeping his eyes straight ahead and moving not a hair, so far as Mr. Fieldpea could tell.

"Very well," Mr. Fieldpea said, "I'll see if that can be arranged. Would you care to come in?"

The mole elected to stand pat, and Mr. Fieldpea went off to find Grenadine, who, as it turned out, was working in the kitchen with her mother. After drying her paws, then, Grenadine placed the heliotrope in a vase, studied the envelope for a bit, opened it and read out, for her parents to hear:

Esteemed Miss Fieldpea,

Please do not count it strange that I, with no letter of introduction, should dare to approach you in such a manner as this. Acknowledging that I am most unworthy to do so, I make bold to announce that I have greatly admired you from a distance and, as I have had no proper opportunity to be introduced to you in the customary way and, moreover, as I have for some time wished most earnestly to make your acquaintance, I beg your indulgence to grant me, if possible, an interview on this very evening.

I await your reply.

Your admiring servant,
LANGSTON PICKEREL

The three Fieldpeas looked at one another for some few moments, thinking this communication strange, indeed, as they had hardly more than seen Mr. Langston Pickerel—and even that from some distance—and thought him to be very unusual, not to say eccentric, and twice Grenadine's age, at least. Grenadine turned somewhat pale at the prospect of his attentions and, at length, was greatly relieved to remember that she was, in fact, previously engaged to spend that very evening with Mr. Predicate Quoty, the author.

She sat down to write a brief reply to Mr. Pickerel's request, intending to express regret that she would not be able to receive him that evening. But after a bit of thought she concluded that she couldn't in all honesty express regret, though she certainly could express appreciation. Here is what she wrote:

Mr. Pickerel,

Thank you, sir, for the lovely bouquet. I must tell you that I am, this evening, obligated by a prior commitment and will not be able to receive you.

Sincerely,
Grenadine Fieldpea

She thought this honest and not unkind. No one could possibly take encouragement from such a communication, she said to herself. She was to learn, however, that with some suitors, neither encouragement nor the lack of it meant anything at all about anything.

Predicate Quoty was an author of some reputation, though not among mice. He made an excellent living writing penny romances for hedgehogs, and, although he considered his stories to be of an inferior genre, they were so popular and remunerative that he didn't see his way clear to not write them. Grenadine found him somewhat shy, but then that seemed to be the way with some of these literary types. And as the two mice made their way, silently, along a pleasant walking path lit by the waning sun, Grenadine said, kindly, "You're very quiet, Mr. Quoty—the more remarkable for a mouse who makes his living expressing himself."

To which Mr. Quoty replied:

> *Those who find the pen a ready sword*
> *To speak whatever thoughts they wish and when*
> *May also find their tongues a ready cord*
> *To snare their thoughts and keep them bound within.*

To which Miss Fieldpea, surprised at the sudden and unexpected appearance of verse in the conversation, but pleased, nonetheless, and almost never without words herself, of course, answered:

> *Then let the words made with your* pen *be on your tongue*
> *And I'll not care they started out in written form.*

Though pen be quick and tongue be slow
The only thing I'll want to know
Is will the heart be warm.

To which Mr. Quoty rejoined:

And should I try my sculptured sentences on you?
And blushing, push them out toward you, there
To hear them clatter out across the cobbled air
And set you mincing through the brittle shards
  Of my week's work?

To which Miss Fieldpea returned:

But if, in spite of all your fears,
Your sentences hold up
And are admired
Indeed, and touch me with their art
Would you not risk a broken thought or two
To reach a mouse's heart?

In answer to which Mr. Quoty said:

Indeed your heart is what I seek to find
Nor would I spare a thousand broken things. . . .

And on and on they went like that until they found themselves back at the burrow, where, as previously arranged, they were joined by Mr. and Mrs. Fieldpea for lemon coolers in the parlor. And whereas Grenadine enjoyed versified conversation, and even found it challenging, still, at the end of the day, so to speak, "challenging" is not quite the same thing as "romantic," is it? But, as, in this particular instance, it provided an evening's protection from Mr. Pickerel's attentions, she found it pleasantly . . . serviceable. Though, as she told this to her mother, later that night, she blushed at the thought of using Mr. Quoty in such a way.

But, alas, this scruple was overwhelmed in the end. For on the following afternoon, the mole was back. He bore a larger and more elaborate bouquet than that of the day before, this one being principally made up of Bristol fairy and meadow rue with a bit of sea lavender thrown in. The salver held another envelope, also white, sealed and addressed to Grenadine, just as on the previous day. Mrs. Fieldpea answered the door, this time, and conveyed both items to Grenadine, who was in the sewing room with her sisters. At the sight of what she was holding, Grenadine looked with a kind of helpless alarm at her mother, paid no attention to the bouquet worth reporting, took the envelope, opened it and read the message, silently, to herself. It said:

Esteemed Miss Fieldpea,

I am so very sorry, though, of course, not surprised, that you were otherwise engaged last evening. Please, then, may I inquire whether the much desired interview might take place on this evening, instead?

I await your reply.

Your admiring servant,
LANGSTON PICKEREL

Having read the note, Grenadine handed it to her sisters, sat down upon the antique burgundy tuffet in her mother's sewing room and cried. Noisily. And upon seeing their sister's suffering and distress, Almandine and Incarnadine Fieldpea sprang into action forthwith. First, with Grenadine's approval, they drafted a brief reply to Mr. Pickerel's note, thanking him for the lovely bouquet and informing him that Miss Fieldpea would not be receiving guests on that particular evening. Then they put on their bonnets, took their parasols and went out. And in consequence of this outing, Grenadine Fieldpea did not lack for evening engagements for several days running.

CHAPTER 12

The Suitors of Grenadine Fieldpea

On Wednesday the mole brought, in one paw, an elegant box of individually wrapped millet seeds and, in the other, a white envelope on the silver tray. Grenadine expressed appreciation for the seeds but let it be known that she was previously engaged for the evening. And, sure enough, at twilight, Stopperfield Toots, editor of *The Tottensea Weekly Noticer,* came calling for her. She was quite well acquainted with Mr. Toots, he having printed a few of her short stories and many of her poems in the *Weekly Noticer.* She had always thought him pleasant enough, mostly good with words and actually a better speller than herself (a thing which she would not have thought possible until he proved it to her one afternoon over a gooseberry spritz). But the poor mouse couldn't rhyme *any*thing, she said to her mother, and his meter was, to her way of thinking, unspeakable.

On Thursday the mole brought a small musical box and an envelope on a salver. Although the gift of the musical box made her uneasy, elevating, as it did, Mr. Pickerel's suit to a more alarming pitch, Grenadine plucked herself up and replied with "The musical box is quite nice, and thank you, of course, but I shall be engaged this evening." And, indeed, Freckeldy Biggles came at the gloaming and took her to a skittles competition where the two of them, as partners, took nearly every single prize. He was very popular, Freckeldy Biggles, being a robust and athletic mouse, an accomplished kegler and more than adequate at rounders, but, as Grenadine told her sisters when she returned that evening, "He has, perhaps, in his life, not read a single book that wasn't required of him."

Friday, still protecting herself from unwanted attentions through another appointment in the continuing series of engagements arranged by her sisters, Grenadine spent the evening with Predicate Quoty's brother, Adverbial Quoty, who wrote poetry but probably shouldn't have.

Adverbial Quoty, a good and sound mouse in so many ways, labored under an unfortunate misunderstanding about his name. Being a bookkeeper and a confessed literalist, Adverbial Quoty felt that, being named Adverbial Quoty, it was his duty to *write* something.

(He needn't have felt such an obligation. So I should pause, here, perhaps, for a brief gloss on field mouse names. They being wonderfully prolific, the ongoing parental duty of field mice to invent names for their issue became something of a challenge—not to say a burden. To help out with this there arose a fashion of naming litters by themes. This is called "thematic littering" and there are a few handbooks on the subject. To be named Predicate Quoty, for example, or Adverbial Quoty—or even Subjunctive Quoty, for that matter—had, therefore, much more to do with the parents' state of exhaustion at the time than with any literary destiny of the new mouse.

If one has never been a very tired mother or father mouse who has barely seen one litter successfully up and out of cribs before another comes along, one may underestimate the relief and convenience which comes with the realization that seven newborn mice could easily be called, say, Sunday, Monday, Tuesday and so forth, or that a litter of six could be quickly named Up, Down, Left, Right, Front and Back and then one could get a little rest. And beyond convenience, the practice became quite original, if not artistic. To name a large litter after leaping lords, for example, or drummers drumming, would certainly never have occurred to me. But, once one gets the hang of it, one sees that it could be done and that, in fact, for very small litters, calling birds could be used, or even French hens.)

Adverbial Quoty was, in Grenadine's view, a mouse of great industry, remarkable success, admirable determination and no literary talent. None.

"What, none at all, dear?" Almandine asked, crestfallen. It was, after all, her idea to have him call, and she felt somewhat responsible.

"As I said," Grenadine answered, pulling her nightdress on over her head.

"But he's only just started writing poetry, I'm told," Almandine said, pulling her own nightdress over her own head. "Perhaps you could encourage him."

"No," Grenadine said firmly, "I couldn't."

"Of course," Almandine said. "I'm sorry to have intruded."

"Not at all, dear," Grenadine said, softening. "He's a

very likable mouse. Really, he is. But he mustn't do poetry, I think."

"Is it his meter, Grenadine?" Almandine asked.

"There's nothing wrong with his meter," Grenadine answered.

"It's the rhymes, then, isn't it?" Almandine sighed. "Why is it they can never rhyme things?"

"No, actually," Grenadine said, "the rhymes are adequate."

"Then . . . ?" Almandine said, helplessly.

"There's more to poetry than rhymes and meters. You should know that, Almandine," Grenadine said, taking up her didactic tone (which Almandine had never liked very much). "A poem must say something worth saying, mustn't it?"

"Was it really as bad as all that?" Almandine asked.

"I leave it to you," Grenadine replied. "He said this:

> *All the city's residents*
> *And twenty college presidents*
> *Could not suppress the evidence*
> *That thou art fair, my love."*

Almandine looked at Grenadine. Grenadine looked at Almandine. They blew out the candle and went to bed.

On Saturday, Martindale DeWiggs asked Grenadine to tea with his family. But that was a bit much.

As the DeWiggses had almost as much money as the Asquith-Berryseeds and as she had no idea what a mouse should wear or say in such company and as she was already toward the ragged end of a rather stressful social whirl, Grenadine Fieldpea buckled at the knees, I'm afraid, and fell across her bed in the grip of a sudden and unexpected onset of the vapors. Almandine and Incarnadine, alarmed and aghast, fanned their sister and insisted on all the customary things: that water be drunk, deep breaths be taken and, above all, that expectations of everything's turning out all right be fully embraced. After remanding their sister to their mother's care, they set forth, again, with bonnets and parasols, in great urgency, to rectify their mistake, if possible, and to do it before the mole arrived on his daily errand.

They were not successful in this. The mole came while they were out.

Utwiler Thipples, the schoolmaster, was a mouse filled right up to his withers with learning and erudition of many kinds to say nothing of his having won the Brittlecakes Normal Prize For Acceptable Literature when quite young. He was a serious mouse, accomplished, a bit didactic, and (having been told that time was of the essence) completely out of breath when he reached the Fieldpea door. After he regained his breath, his composure and his voice well enough to extend his invitation, Grenadine said to him, "Thank you ever so much, Mr. Thipples, for your kindness in coming under these circumstances, but I regret to tell you that I am already engaged for this evening."

Indeed she was.

When the mole had come, earlier that afternoon, her mother had insisted on writing a note, herself, to Mr. Pickerel, informing him that Miss Fieldpea was indisposed and unable to receive any guests whatsoever, either that evening or for some indefinite time to come. But Grenadine wouldn't have it. She had recovered quickly from her swoon and was uncommonly vexed with herself for such an appalling lapse of self-control. Moreover, she was determined to receive this unpleasantly persistent suitor once and for all and be done with it. Flushed with agitation, then, she sat and wrote: "You may call upon me at six o'clock but I would be pleased if you would send no more gifts." She threw that away and wrote: "You may come at six, this evening. The brooch is lovely but quite unnecessary." After she tore that up she wrote, "Come at six. Thanks for the brooch." And she gave that one to the mole.

At six o'clock, then, Langston Pickerel came to the door and Mr. Fieldpea, who knew a thing or two about the world, showed him to the parlor with warmth and courtesy, to be sure, but with no more to-do than he had shown a Mr. Quoty or a Mr. Biggles or a Mr. Toots. When Grenadine appeared she was astonished, of course (as nearly everyone was at seeing Langston Pickerel up close for the first time), but determined not to show it. Still it was hard. What kind of expression would you have had on your face if you had dis-covered, standing in your parlor, a creature in a powdered wig and postillion boots, wearing a maroon cloak over a blue waistcoat and fronted with a ruffled something or other—a jabot, I think? And if he had been wearing white silk breeches and if, on a table beside him, there was an ivory-headed cane alongside a tricorn that had a silver medallion on it and long striped feathers that you had never seen before, and if he had been holding a large bouquet of pearly everlasting inter-spersed with Siberian bugloss, you, too, might have remained cool and unblinking only with the most dedicated effort and resolution.

Still, she did it—stayed cool, I mean, and didn't blink, though, in all fairness, she did have her face half hidden behind the folding fan which she had borrowed from Incarnadine. But when she extended her paw the way she had read about ladies doing in books and Mr. Pickerel took it in his own and kissed it and then said things to her which she had only read about in those same books and said them with an elegant French accent, Grenadine thought to herself that, after all, an exotic evening with a mysterious and chivalrous stranger might provide at least an interesting diary entry for the evening, if not material for a short story or two!

After Mr. Pickerel had gone, Almandine and Incarnadine, breathless and wide-eyed, cornered their sister in the hallway and inquired about the evening.

"It was all very pleasant," Grenadine said, archly. "He's been to the Continent, you know."

"And . . . ?" said Almandine.

"And what, dear?" Grenadine said, yawning and pretending to appear puzzled by her sisters' curiosity.

"Grenadine!" Incarnadine said. "You were in there for an *hour!*"

"Well . . . give me a moment, then. Let's see, we spoke of weather, and a bit about literature. He quoted me a poem. No, two poems. And—oh!—did I say that he asked me to accompany him to the Tottensea Burrows Midsummer's Night Fancy Dress Cotillion Ball?" said Grenadine, with a straight face, and she ran away toward their room. Her sisters screeched and chased her down the hallway, the three of them laughing boisterously. In their room, then, they put their heads together and Grenadine told them about Langston Pickerel.

All eyes and ears, Incarnadine said, "He was genteel and romantic, then."

"Oh, Incarnadine, he was positively Byronic! He told me I reminded him of an actress he once knew in Budapest, except that she was taller, he said, and not so beautiful."

"Budapest!" said Incarnadine. "An actress! You didn't believe it?"

"No, actually," Grenadine answered. "But he did *say* it, didn't he, and I require nothing more than that for my diary!" They laughed and Almandine asked her if she was actually going to the ball with him.

"Oh, most certainly. It could keep me in story material for the rest of summer don't you think?" They all agreed about this and went off to tell their mother. That turned out to be somewhat disappointing, however, as their mother was less than enthusiastic about the project.

"But, Mother," Grenadine said, "it was more or less irresistible."

Mrs. Fieldpea worked at her needlepoint, and without looking up said, "Well, my dear, you are a grown mouse, and entitled to make these decisions for yourself."

"Was it quite wrong of me to accept, then?"

"My thought would have been this," Mrs. Fieldpea said, putting down her work. "If you think Mr. Pickerel sincere, it is unbecoming of you to treat the invitation cynically. If you think him insincere, then no good can come of your involvement with him on any account."

Grenadine's diary entry was interesting that evening. But it was interesting in a different way than she had thought it would be.

CHAPTER 13

Mrs. Pockets' Difficult Guest

For a very small mouse, Farnaby Pockets liked excitement. His mother, Mrs. Proserpine Pockets, noticed this and she used to say to him, as he tried to stand quite still while she buttoned his jerkin, "Now Farnaby, there are very many wonderful things in this world, but not all of them are exciting. Do you understand that, dear?" "I think so," he would say, cheerfully. He was a good little field mouse and his mother loved him very much but she wasn't sure that he did understand about this excitement business.

As Mrs. Pockets and Farnaby were very poor, they took in boarders to make ends meet. When they first came to Tottensea Burrows, Mrs. Pockets found an old inn which had been abandoned and which she thought might be fixed up into a reasonable boardinghouse. She swept it out, scrubbed it up, whitewashed the walls, mended the thatch and put a little sign in the front window that said ROOMS.

There was already a big sign. The big sign hung out over the front door and said THE BRAMBLES on it because that had been the name of the old inn. It squeaked a little when

the wind blew, being a swinging sign that hadn't been properly cared for, and it needed new paint. But there were so many other things in the place that needed attention even more than the sign that although Mrs. Pockets, on every evening in which there was a breeze, said to herself, as she fell wearily into her bed, "I must do something about that sign . . . just as soon as we think of a name for the boardinghouse," in the end, she didn't. She didn't do anything about the sign and she didn't think of a new name, either.

But, if one thinks about it, the wind doesn't blow very hard in Tottensea, after all. So the squeaking isn't all that shocking. And as for the old paint, some mice (probably out of kindness) told her that they thought it had a pleasant antique look about it. In any event, the boardinghouse went on being called The Brambles and the sign over its door went on squeaking a little, when the wind blew, and never got repainted. But hardly anyone ever complained about the sign. The guests seemed to like The Brambles and were generally a cheerful lot. Except for Mr. Neversmythe.

Mr. Neversmythe came to The Brambles in a pouring rain, in the middle of the night, and he made a great din of it, too. Farnaby was in bed when the uproar began, but, of course, a young mouse couldn't be expected to stay in bed through a thing like that. By the time he found his mother she had already lit a candle, put a robe over her nightclothes and was saying, so as to be heard (if possible) above the pounding and noise being put upon their door, "Yes, yes. I'm coming. Just a moment, please. Goodness!" When she finally did get to the door she was almost afraid to open it as things were being said on the other side of it—things, like "One ought not to be treated in such a way on a night like this!" and "False notices I calls it" and "'Rooms' it says, as plain as ever I saw the word." But open it she did and found nearly the wettest creature she had ever seen standing right in front of her, wearing a yellow sou'wester and a great yellow mackintosh and Wellington boots right up to his knees—none of them doing him any good, whatsoever, he being at least as wet on the inside as he was on the outside—and as soon as the door came open he said, "All right, you've opened the door, I suppose. What's to be done now?"

"Well, you must come in, of course!" Mrs. Pockets said. So in he came and a considerable amount of weather with him. Immediately he was inside he began sputtering and wheezing and, with both paws, slapping great amounts of water off his raincoat and right onto Mrs. Pockets' clean floor as if it were of the utmost importance that everything about him be made completely dry as soon as possible and never mind that anything else in the world might become slightly damp in consequence of it.

"Goodness!" Mrs. Pockets said again, feeling, perhaps, as if the rainstorm itself had come into her parlor and was now about to ask her for a room.

Farnaby Pockets watched all this with very wide eyes and, as their guest seemed quite occupied with his own affairs and not likely to notice anything else that was happening in the general area, he made bold to ask his mother, albeit very quietly, and in a discreet whisper, "What *is* he?"

"I'm not certain, darling," his mother whispered back, "but I think he may be a bog lemming. We mustn't ask, of course. It would be rude."

"Oh," Farnaby whispered. And then he waited as long as possible and when he absolutely could stand it not a moment longer he whispered again to his mother, "What's that thing hanging off him?"

"I believe it's called a cutlass, dear," his mother whispered.

Mr. Neversmythe proved to be a very difficult guest. He was not only loud and blustery, he was also bad tempered and frightening to the other guests. When asked about his occupation, he would usually say, very noisily, that he was a frontier numismatist, and a cracking good one at that. And, though he might well have collected coins somewhere out along the rough edges of civilization, it was greatly suspected by myself that he actually did this collecting at the point of a sword and with motives quite other than those of antiquarian interest. But, of course, I am a bird. Actually, though, the field mice may have suspected it, as well, for though they are kind-spirited and have even been accused of being excessively inclined to give benefits of doubt, they are not stupid.

Another unpleasant thing about Mr. Neversmythe was that he was often greatly in arrears in the matter of paying for his room and his meals. This caused distress to Mrs. Pockets. And when she would sometimes gather herself and determine that she simply must do her duty and ask her unpleasant guest about this matter, and after a bad night of worrying about when, exactly, she would do this and, what, exactly, she would say, and when, after watching diligently and finding an opportunity, somehow, as he was returning to his room after breakfast, or coming in from one of his long walks in the afternoon, Mrs. Proserpine Pockets would say something like, "Ahem, sir, about your fees . . . ," he would say, noisily, and in a very cross manner, "Oh, very well!" and then go to his room and slam the door and not pay them.

He kept, in his room, a small chest or locker, and, though no one had ever seen into it, one might have been forgiven for assuming that it contained his coin collection, or at least a part of it. It might also have been assumed that the chest was always kept locked as Mr. Neversmythe was not to be seen in public without a small brass key dangling in plain sight from a thread around his neck.

For many days, Farnaby thought it quite exciting to keep an eye on Mr. Neversmythe. But he was very careful about it—only looking at him around the edges of doors or through banister rails or, once, from under a wing chair. Watching from under the chair proved to be not so good because Mr. Neversmythe came and sat on the chair while Farnaby was under it. And he sat there for a long time before he said, "All right, Pockets, bring yourself up straight and let's have a look at you."

Farnaby was very scared, but he crawled right out from under the chair and stood up in front of Mr. Neversmythe, who said, "Aye, and so I can see you're a watcher, then, and I'll be having some use for a watcher, it's true. But you see here,

Pockets, I'll have none of your spyin' and that's a fact—least not on *me,* do y'understand. If there's spyin' to be done—an' I'm not sayin' there is and I'm not sayin' there ain't—then I'll be tellin' you what there is to be spyin' about and who there is to be spyin' upon. Do I make meself clear, Pockets?"

Of course, Farnaby Pockets was much too frightened to say whether Mr. Neversmythe made himself clear or whether he didn't. At that very moment all Farnaby was thinking about was that he wanted to be somewhere else besides where he was. He wasn't, though. He was standing right there exactly where he was standing. And to his way of thinking, standing right there was slightly too exciting.

"Now, listen up, Pockets, and be keen about it," Mr. Neversmythe went on, all the while poking a long index claw right into Farnaby's chest so hard that it hurt. "You keeps your ears open, Pockets, and there'll be a silver mouseshilling in it for you if you hear anything about a Saracen's knife with three baubles on it. Do y'understand me, Pockets?"

Farnaby nodded that he did and that was partly true. He knew what ears were and mouseshillings and knives. And he thought he knew what baubles were. He just didn't have the slightest idea about the other word.

So, that evening, Farnaby, having served the guests their casseroles in the dining room, and having poured their drinks for them and having given them their desserts when they wanted them and having cleared their tables and swept the dining room when they were finished, and having washed all the crockery and cutlery and skillets and pipkins and pots and skimmers and ladles, and having dried all such things and put them away carefully in their proper places so that his mother could find them when next she wanted them, and while sitting at the little table in the back of the kitchen, eating his own casserole, said to his mother, "What are Saracens?"

And then his mother, having cleaned the front hallway and the parlor and all the guest rooms from top to bottom, and having swept and dusted the front stairs and the back hallway and having washed practically every linen in the place including their own things as well as the sheets and towels from all the guest rooms and having hung them on the clothesline and, when they were dry, having brought them in and ironed those that needed ironing and folded those that needed folding, and having rushed to the market to buy chicory and rose hips and cauliflower and cinnamon and several kinds of cheese, and having rushed home with it all and having put away in the pantry those things which she didn't need at the moment, and having used the rest to cook a savory casserole, and having sat down at the little table in the back of the kitchen for just a moment to eat a bite of her own casserole before jumping up to prepare some foods for breakfast the next day, said to Farnaby, "What are *what,* dear?"

"Saracens," Farnaby said. "And does any one of them have a knife with three baubles on it?"

"I don't exactly know about Saracens, Farnaby," Mrs. Pockets said, "though I have heard the word and, yes, I have heard it in connection with a certain knife . . . ," and she stopped for some reason and looked intently at her little mouse, "but may I first know why you are asking me this?"

"It's for a mouseshilling, Mother," Farnaby said, somewhat impatiently, continuing to eat his casserole.

"Is it indeed? And how might that be, dear?"

"Well," Farnaby said, carefully, "actually . . . a creature said that he would give me a mouseshilling if ever I heard of such a thing."

"I see," said Mrs. Pockets, continuing to eat *her* casserole. "What sort of creature, Farnaby?"

"Umm . . . a lemming, I believe," Farnaby said.

"A bog lemming, perhaps."

"We *think* he may be a bog lemming, yes," said Farnaby, giving much attention to the last bits of the casserole scattered around various locations in his bowl.

"Hmm, that would be Mr. Neversmythe, I expect."

Farnaby said nothing, devoted as he was, at the moment, to orts of casserole.

"Mr. Neversmythe, then, promised you a mouseshilling if ever you heard of a Saracen's knife with three baubles on it. Is that right, Farnaby?" Mrs. Pockets asked.

"Yes," her little mouse said very softly.

Mrs. Pockets looked up from her bowl, though not at Farnaby, and said, "Oh dear." She then fetched a piece of paper from a drawer, wrote something on it with a pen, placed it in an envelope, wrote a name on the envelope, sealed it and said, "Now, in the morning, dear, you must take this to Mr. Twofolding-Wetstraw."

Farnaby's eyes went suddenly wide. "Oh, Mother, may I take it now, please? I'm told The Silver Claw at night is ever such a wonderful place."

Mrs. Pockets looked totally dubious about such an idea.

"Oh, please, Mother. I'll be ever so quick about it. I'll come back straightaway. You'll see. May I go just this once?"

And when he thought he saw that his mother was actually weakening, he said, without wasting another moment, "To see what it's like and all. Just to see what it's like. Nothing more than that."

Mrs. Pockets hesitated for one split mousesecond too long, I think, and Farnaby, seeing that a tiny window of opportunity had unexpectedly opened before him, said, rapidly, and in a rather jumbled fashion, not having the advantage of advanced planning, "Perhaps it isn't. At night, I mean. Wonderful. Perhaps it's, after all, completely dull."

And with his mother *still* not looking completely satisfied, he hurried on, "And if it *is* very dull, then I should like very much to know that, Mother. Because . . . because I've heard . . . that it isn't."

Then Mrs. Pockets, most certainly against her better judgment, and not at all knowing exactly why she was doing it, nevertheless heard herself saying, while pointing directly at Farnaby's nose, "You must *not tarry,* do you hear?"

With the most urgent seriousness, Farnaby assured his mother that he would not even THINK of tarrying in a case like this. And off he went to The Silver Claw. But if Mrs. Pockets had known what kind of creatures had just arrived in Tottensea Burrows that very day and who would be at The Silver Claw that very night I can assure you that she would not by any means have let her little mouse go over there! Most certainly not!

CHAPTER 14

The Silver Claw
at Night

The Silver Claw was a public house, or, as field mice often called it, a "pub," which was an establishment where beverages of a certain kind were sold and consumed. An animal could also get a bit of nourishment there if he wished—a lively bit of spinach, perhaps, or even brussels sprouts if times were good. It was sometimes true of field mouse pubs that there were also rooms which a creature could rent if it needed a place to stay.

Farnaby Pockets had been many times inside The Silver Claw in his young life. Once a week, his mother baked very delicious pastries and sold them to some of the shops in Tottensea Burrows. It was Farnaby's job to pack the pastries into a straw basket, and do it very carefully so that none of them would be broken or smashed, and then to cover them with a red-and-white-check cloth to keep the dust off them and then to deliver them to the shops that had ordered them.

Farnaby loved pastry day because his mother would always set aside a special pastry for her little delivery mouse which he would be allowed to eat immediately he returned from his toils. But he mustn't hurry his rounds in order to have his treat all the sooner. Of course not. He must put on his carroty red corduroy cap which just matched his carroty red corduroy knickerbockers and go off and do it in the amount of time that was fitting. This meant that if you had been in Tottensea Burrows on almost any Monday afternoon, you could have seen a polite and well-dressed little mouse coming along carrying a straw basket of pastries and, just as he passed by you, could have heard his carroty red corduroy knickerbockers going whiff, whiff, whiff at an entirely suitable rate of speed.

But while Farnaby Pockets had been many times inside The Silver Claw, he had never been inside The Silver Claw at night. It was so different that for a moment he wondered if he had taken himself into the wrong place by mistake. He had never seen so many different kinds of creatures in the same room. Why, he couldn't by any means have named even all the different kinds of mice he saw there, to say nothing of the voles and the rats, the moles and the conies, a small hedgehog, I daresay, and one little animal that someone said might even have been a shrew—though it had such a large hat pulled so low over its eyes that no one could be sure, and, in case it *was* a shrew, I can tell you for certain that no one there was about to ask it!

The patrons of The Silver Claw that night were all eating or drinking or smoking clay pipes with long stems or throwing darts or playing at backgammon or draughts or cards or else saying something or listening to something that someone else was saying. Most of them sat around tables lit by straw-covered bottles with candles in them or by lanterns hanging from crossbeams in the ceiling. At one end of the room was a

counter with a few customers in front of it and a
busy mouse behind it doing things with ket-
tles and jugs and flasks and bottles as well as
with kegs and barrels and casks
which had spigots sticking out
near the bottoms of them. A
row of pegs, on the wall oppo-
site, held caps and hats and there
was a brolly alongside a mackintosh or two. There was a fireplace
that had a mantel with a clock and a
vase holding some unhappy flowers
that badly wanted to be replaced—
though Farnaby might have wondered how long
a vase of flowers *could* have been happy and con-
tented in a room as hot and stuffy and smoky as The Silver
Claw at night.

Farnaby saw a face that he knew across the room and
began to make his way through this noisy, busy, elbowy place.
And because there was hardly enough space to squeeze
between the tables and chairs, he passed much too close to
four or five ship rats hunched together over a table, speaking
in low voices and watching him with suspicion. They
weren't looking at him with suspicion for any particular reason, I think. Ship rats, I'm told, look at everyone with suspicion! In any event, suddenly and without warning, the rat
with the gold ring in his ear and a patch over one eye
reached, quick as a snake, and laid an iron grip on Farnaby's
shoulder. "What'll ya be doin' here, boy?" the rat said, but in
a room so noisy that only those close by could have heard

him. "Who sent ya to be spyin' on poor simple creatures what only want to raise an honest elbow with a few good friends? Eh?" And the iron grip tightened till Farnaby thought he might cry.

"Why no one, sir! I'm not spyin' on no one at all, sir," said Farnaby Pockets, frightened quite beyond all the good grammar that Mr. Utwiler Thipples The Schoolmaster had ever taught him.

"Aye, and I'll not have ya lyin' to me, boy," said the rat, thrusting a black claw in Farnaby's face. "No' a word of it, d'ya hear?" And he held tightly to Farnaby with the one paw while he took a pull at his ale with the other. He wiped his mouth on a dirty brown sleeve and said, "All right, off with ya, then." And he pointed the claw at Farnaby's face again, "And no more snoopin' about or I'll be havin' a look at the gizzard of ya with a rusty blade, I will, or me name's not Frenchie Grimwott—which it *is*." And his one eye glared at Farnaby as if it might pop right out of its socket. "Begone with ya!" And the iron grip having released him, at last, Farnaby lurched away and scrambled off hurriedly and was not to be looking back even when he heard an explosion of laughter from the rats' table.

Farnaby was proud that he hadn't cried for the rat. Not really *cried*, I mean. It's true that his eyes were watery and his vision a bit blurred as he moved on through the room, but some of those tears came from the tobacco smoke that had stung his eyes from the moment he came in the door. And though there was still trouble getting through the crowd, with things being said to him like "That'll be me foot, lad!" or "It's me back yer puttin' yer elbow into, sir, if you don't mind!" at least no one else took hold of him or said anything to him about looking at his gizzard.

You can imagine, I think, what a great relief it was to Farnaby when he finally heard a friendly voice that he knew. "Why Master Pockets, as I breathe," said Mr. Denslow Twofolding-Wetstraw, proprietor of The Silver Claw. Though he was working hard at that moment serving his customers, the old mouse stopped nonetheless to give kind attention to a young mouse on a mission. He had a towel over one arm, Mr. Twofolding-Wetstraw did, and he was holding a tray full of mugs and cups and tankards high over his head with the other and was huffing and puffing a little as he said, "And it's not even Monday, I believe."

"No sir, Mr. Twofolding-Wetstraw," said Farnaby Pockets, but said it in an ordinary quiet field mouse kind of voice, which of course could not at all be heard above the noise of The Silver Claw at night. So he said it again, only louder, and Mr. Twofolding-Wetstraw bent down as low as he could to try to hear, bearing in mind that the tray of mugs and cups and tankards must still be held as high as possible on account of other creatures' heads and things. So Farnaby Pockets was obliged to say a third time, "No sir, Mr. Twofolding-Wetstraw. I've not come about the pastries this time."

"Not about the pastries, is it? Very well, then, come with me," said Mr. Twofolding-Wetstraw, motioning Farnaby to follow him, which, of course, he did and ended up at a little rolltop desk in the back corner of the kitchen of The Silver Claw, which, though a considerably quieter place, was not a bit less busy with waiters and cooks bustling over here and over there and hardly slowing down even for a mouseminute.

"Now then, Master Pockets, of what service can I be to a fine young fellow like yourself on a busy evening like this," said the tired mouse, who had put down his tray of cups and mugs and tankards and sat himself at his desk and was wiping his brow with the towel.

"Well, Mr. Twofolding-Wetstraw, I'm very sorry to trouble you at such a busy time but I have a message for Mr. Pickerel from Mrs. Pockets and she said that it was very important that I give it to you, sir." And Farnaby held out the envelope.

"Mr. Pickerel, is it?" Mr. Twofolding-Wetstraw said, taking the envelope and looking at it and rubbing his chin with a paw and frowning ever so slightly. "Hmm. Yes. You're right, of course. 'Mr. Langston Pickerel' it says, right here in plain writing. Well, now let me see, then. You must tell your dear mother, sir, that I can't promise her anything," and he looked at Farnaby over his spectacles and pointed one claw at nothing in particular. "He does keep rooms here, it's true, but still, in all, one doesn't see him very often, you understand. Mr. Pickerel comes, you see, and Mr. Pickerel goes. It could be days. It could be weeks. But one will do what one can." And he unlocked the desk and placed the envelope in a little compartment inside it. Then Mr. Denslow Twofolding-Wetstraw gave young Master Pockets a cup of chocolate which was very sweet and very hot. Farnaby thanked his host, politely, drank the chocolate as fast as he reasonably could (it being so hot), fervently hoping all the while that it would not be counted against him as tarrying, and then he hurried right home to his mother. Straightaway.

CHAPTER 15

Preparations for a Ball

The Tottensea Burrows Midsummer's Night Fancy Dress Cotillion Ball was, beyond question, the premier social event of the field mouse season. All Tottensea was in a flutter over it for weeks.

The Fieldpea burrow, along with many others, stirred mightily at such a time, for fancy dress, itself, was there being extensively planned, perpetually discussed, and, in the end, painstakingly constructed. Many of Mr. Fieldpea's meals were peppered with words of great mystery to him, words such as furbelows, for example, and flounces. Pelerines were spoken of openly at table. Bandeaux were mentioned, whatever they were.

The Fieldpea girls, for fellowship, brought their projects to the sitting room after dinner, so that as Mr. Fieldpea sat in his chair reading *The Tottensea Weekly Noticer* or, it might have been, *The Rodent's Digest,* all about him swirled a sea of the most intense activity—fabrics being snipped, needles threaded, hems stitched, digits pricked, patience tested, mistakes realized, patterns referred to, tears shed and gowns finally and triumphantly made!

One evening, amid the stir and bustle of these doings, Incarnadine came into the sitting room to show off her new dancing slippers.

"Oh, Incarnadine, they're lovely!" Almandine said.

"Do you like them? The buckles are actually silver, I believe. With luck, I shall dance the quadrille with Merchanty Swift in these," Incarnadine said, rehearsing a turn from that dance.

"That *will* take a bit of luck," Grenadine said, not looking up, "since Merchanty Swift doesn't attend balls."

"Merchanty Swift doesn't attend anything," Almandine said, with a sigh. "And it isn't fair."

"You are both altogether too pessimistic, is my opinion," sniffed Incarnadine. "These things can change. A mouse can be smitten more than once. Parsalina Smarts said that."

"Did she, indeed?" asked Almandine.

"She did," replied Incarnadine, "and I'm inclined to agree with her."

"And who may we expect to do this . . . re-smiting, dear?" Almandine asked. "Would it be Parsalina Smarts, then? Or yourself, perhaps?"

At the word "re-smiting," Incarnadine was quite unable to maintain a straight face. And as Grenadine began to invent a conjugation for the verb "to re-smite" the discussion was overtaken by snickers and then guffaws. By the time she had attained the form "we shall have been re-smitten" they were all more or less seized of laughter and Mr. Fieldpea looked up, briefly, from his article to suggest that, after all, the new verb might have to be abandoned for the sake of getting one's breath.

On the day of the ball, anticipation and preparations of many kinds reached elevated levels across all Tottensea. Proserpine Pockets, on that day, was rather up to her ears, so to speak, and somewhat behind schedule in the making of pastries and relishes for the celebrated event. And so when she heard, behind her, the sound of walnut bits falling off a counter, striking the floor and shooting off in many directions, and when she turned in time to see Farnaby badly overreaching to lick up a spill of icing sugar and saw that the walnut bowl had been overturned because of that overreaching, she fell out of temper and, rounding upon her mouseling, turned him out-of-doors. "Farnaby Pockets!" she said sharply, "you are quite underfoot, my dear!"

The mouseling, embarrassed, if not chagrined, went outside and climbed up into a rhododendron for the comfort of it.

Shortly thereafter, Miss Middlechippers, the Pocketses' elderly neighbor, appeared in Mrs. Pockets' kitchen, wide-eyed and leaning on her cane for a moment to catch her breath until she could actually say the words: "Mr. Pickerel! He's coming! *Here,* I think!"

Mrs. Pockets said, "Well, that's all right, dear, we'll just let him come." And after Miss Middlechippers, in a state, fled out the back door, Mrs. Pockets smoothed her apron and glanced quickly at the large brass tray which hung like a mirror on the kitchen wall near the pantry. She went to answer a knock at the front door, thinking as she went, perhaps, that of all the times for Langston Pickerel to choose to call upon her, this might be the least convenient one possible!

She opened the door to a creature who, no matter how many times one had seen him, was always somewhat surprising. This time—gracious!—he was in a white periwig topped by a plumed cavalier hat and he wore a ruffled collar under a blue frock coat, beet-red breeches and great, flaring jackboots! And he was heavily armed, at that. There was a rapier on his hip!

He swept the hat off his wigged head and bowed deeply before her. He thanked her most kindly for her letter, and asked if it would be at all convenient for her to take him to the room of the Mr. Neversmythe in question. And though it was not even approximately convenient, she was much too polite to say so, and took him. After a genteel knock on Mr. Neversmythe's door was answered by a gruff and blustery voice from inside the room saying, "Who's there? I might ask!" Mr. Pickerel said, "Thank you, Madame, for your trouble," and offered her a coin, which she respectfully declined. He then opened the door and disappeared into Mr. Neversmythe's room.

Mrs. Pockets had hardly reached the end of the hallway before that very door burst open with a loud noise and Mr. Neversmythe, himself, fled from his room, right past her, down the stairs and out the front door with such a hurry and bustle that hats flew off their pegs as he went by and one or two gimcracks fell off a shelf and broke into pieces so small that they were quite beyond mending. Mr. Pickerel walked calmly from Mr. Neversmythe's room, sheathing his weapon, and with a slight bow before the astonished Mrs. Pockets, said, "If you would be so kind as to send me a statement of all Mr. Neversmythe's charges, including these regrettable damages, you may be certain that all his debts shall be paid to you in full. I am most distressed for the trouble he has caused you, Madame, and I believe that you shall not see him again." He pulled on a pair of immaculate white gloves and adjusted them meticulously. "I shall send someone for his things," he said.

Farnaby had seen Mr. Pickerel go into The Brambles—though, owing to his position high in the rhododendron, he had not been seen by Mr. Pickerel. He was very interested in something on Mr. Pickerel's person. And as Farnaby perched there and pondered what he had seen, he was startled by Mr. Neversmythe, fleeing out the door and away at high speed. Moments later, Mr. Pickerel, himself, came back out and Farnaby got another look at the thing most interesting to him. It wasn't the white periwig and it wasn't the jackboots. It wasn't even the rapier. It was hanging from Langston Pickerel's patent leather belt, all right, but it was much shorter than the rapier and it was curved in a peculiar way. It looked, too, Farnaby thought, as if it might be jeweled.

When the pastries and relishes were finished, Mrs. Pockets went to the door and summoned Farnaby to help her deliver them. But there was no Farnaby there to be summoned. She called out the front. She called out the back. She checked with Miss Middlechippers. There was no Farnaby.

Put out with herself and put out with a bilberry tart for breaking right in half when it was picked up and put out with Farnaby and, most of all, worried about why Farnaby was not where he was supposed to be, and somehow managing three baskets and two trays as best she could by herself, Proserpine Pockets set out for Tottensea Hall. As she walked along she calmed herself with the thought that no place in all Tottensea Burrows was as exciting at that moment as that very place to which she was going. If Farnaby had been irresistibly drawn to someplace that afternoon, she reasoned, it would surely be Tottensea Hall.

She was certainly right about the excitement! The hall was hopping with activity of all kinds. There were mice at the ceiling: festooning everything that could be festooned—with garlands being made to travel from every chandelier to every cornice board and back again. There were mice on the floor: putting beeswax on it and polishing, polishing, polishing. There were mice in between: arranging flowers, replacing candles in the chandeliers, rehearsing music, laying out refreshments. There was all that and more, but there was no Farnaby.

Emmalina Fieldpea was there putting out her oat-seed cakes and no, dear, she hadn't seen Farnaby all day. Octavia Baggs was there rehearsing with the rest of the Cotillion Ensemble and she had not seen Farnaby, either, though she did go on to say that Opportune was getting very near to completing the Mousewriter and had told her that he might even try a curlicue or two that very afternoon. Was it possible that Farnaby had heard about that and gone to see it done? She didn't think so, Proserpine Pockets said, but she would check.

After checking at the Baggses', she went to ask Merchanty Swift if he had seen her mouse. Clementine Nickelpenny said that Mr. Swift was away on business and not expected until later that evening and, no, she hadn't seen Farnaby, either, going on to point out that Proserpine looked frightfully tired and was she sure she wouldn't come in for a moment, dear, and have a nice cup of tea in the interest of strength. No, Proserpine Pockets would not come in. She would go home. Wherever he had gone, she said, Farnaby would surely be at home by now.

But he wasn't.

CHAPTER 16

The Tottensea Burrows Midsummer's Night Fancy Dress Cotillion Ball

On the night of The Tottensea Burrows Midsummer's Night Fancy Dress Cotillion Ball, Tottensea Hall was thrillingly ablaze with light! And to this luminous place all sorts of field mice came in their glory. Luminous were they themselves— all splendid in brilliant gowns, dignified tunics and colorful waistcoats. Greetings were exchanged, admiration declared and affection expressed. Fair mice were duly escorted about the room by gallant other mice. The refreshments were refreshing and the merriment flowed as the punch. Visiting and nibbling and sipping went on throughout the hall.

The Mayor was master of ceremonies at the ball and he acquitted himself well enough—as well as a bachelor could do on an occasion like that, I suppose. Everyone would have thought it really grand if he had had a beautiful companion to share the honors of the evening. But, of course, mice can't have everything.

Sir Rotherham always made a good impression at these

events. He used the gold-rimmed monocle that evening, and in his morning coat and striped trousers he was very well presented.

The General, on the other hand, was in some discomfiture in the matter of appearance throughout the evening. One or other of the collars of his uniform, in some unsymmetrical way, seemed determined to raise itself above its counterpart. He was seen often at the mirror, attempting to reconcile the collars by manipulation, pushing this one up and the other one down, or after closer inspection, pushing this one down and the other one up. Clementine Nickelpenny could have fixed the problem in a mouseminute with a sprinkle of water and a hot flatiron. But she was at home in her bed, wasn't she?—propped up on pillows with a nice cup of tea, rereading *Millicent's Surprised Heart* and dabbing at her eyes, from time to time, with a silk handkerchief.

Umpteen Weeks was at home, as well. Much too old for that sort of nonsense, he would have said. Miss Middlechippers was at home, too, and almost as old as he was—but she certainly wouldn't have called the ball nonsense! It's just that she hadn't been asked.

Glendowner Fieldpea was at the ball with two of his

daughters. Leacock Hardesty The Younger was there and busy getting his name onto Parsalina Smarts' dance card. Warburton Nines Who Once Lifted A Cat was certainly not there and never would have been. Octavia Baggs was, and was warming up her fipple flute. Opportune Baggs stayed at home with the children and was making curlicues, actually, at that moment.

And anxious and distraught, as you can imagine, Proserpine Pockets was at home, too—watching and waiting for Farnaby to turn up.

At eight o'clock, exactly, the Mayor gave a nod and the Tottensea Burrows Cotillion Ensemble played the quadrille.

Incarnadine Fieldpea danced it with Freckledy Biggles. Almandine Fieldpea mirrored the same figures with Stopperfield Toots. When the two sisters came together at the center of the floor, in the order of the movements, Almandine whispered rather urgently, "Where's Grenadine?" Incarnadine lifted her shoulders in reply as they moved away from each other. When they advanced again Almandine hissed, "She's missing the quadrille!" Incarnadine hissed back, "Yes, dear. I know!" and retreated once more in obedience to the dance.

After the quadrille, Incarnadine, from behind her folding fan, was just whispering to Almandine, "I don't care whether Freckledy Biggles reads books or not! Did you see him *dance*?" when Parsalina Smarts came up to them and more or less demanded to know where Grenadine was. Hazeltine Smarts came up to them, as well, visibly disappointed. Where was Langston Pickerel? She wanted to see him.

All at once, every mouse in the place seemed to be turning to look at the entrance of the hall. Someone had just come in.

Whisperings rose up to become murmurings—with amazement not far behind. The Fieldpea sisters pressed through for a better view, relieved that, at least, Grenadine would be in time for the minuet and eager to see what on earth Langston Pickerel *would* wear on a night like this. But it wasn't Grenadine Fieldpea. It wasn't Langston Pickerel. It was Merchanty Swift! What else would happen!

Grenadine Fieldpea was not to be found dancing a quadrille or a minuet or a galop or any other thing at The Tottensea Burrows Midsummer's Night Fancy Dress Cotillion Ball because Grenadine Fieldpea was to be found at home, that evening, playing gin rummy with her mother while dressed in a gown which had taken her two weeks to make from a very expensive material which had cost most of her savings to buy.

Her mother said, "It *is* an elegant gown, Grenadine. Very handsomely made."

"Thank you, Mother," Grenadine said crisply and without smiling, "but I must tell you that I feel somewhat overdressed for a card game. Gin."

"Oh, dear. Gin it is," Mrs. Fieldpea said and laid down her cards, counted the points, recorded the score, shuffled the pack and dealt.

"I don't want that," Grenadine said, referring to the four of clubs her mother had just turned up.

"Very well, then. I may have some use for it," Mrs. Fieldpea said, taking the card for herself. "What do you suppose has happened, dear?" she asked, discarding the nine of diamonds.

"I'm sure I haven't the slightest idea, Mother," Grenadine replied, drawing a card and discarding the knave of hearts, "but I am quite humiliated and wish never to hear the name Langston Pickerel again."

"I quite understand, dear," Mrs. Fieldpea said, taking the knave and discarding the queen of spades.

Grenadine drew a card. "Perhaps he fell into a ditch," she said, with a bit more passion than she intended. She then discarded the seven of diamonds, which her mother took straightaway. "Mother, must you take every single card I lay down!"

"But they're such lovely cards, aren't they?" her mother said. "Gin."

"Oh!" Grenadine said, collapsing her spread of cards with something very close to a show of temper. She recovered quickly, however, and shuffled the pack while her mother wrote down the score. Then, expressing a new thought as she dealt, Grenadine said, "You don't suppose he did it deliberately?"

"I shouldn't like to think that of anyone!" Mrs. Fieldpea replied.

"Nor should I," said Grenadine, with middling sincerity, and turned up the deuce of hearts, which her mother took, immediately. "We must try to think happier thoughts, then," Grenadine said. "Perhaps he merely broke his leg." Her mother looked up without speaking and discarded the ten of spades. "Or has measles," Grenadine went on, "or got himself arrested for some terrible crime." She took the ten and discarded the king of clubs. "Smuggling, perhaps."

Her mother drew a card and discarded another.

"Yes, that would be it, I believe," Grenadine said. "He was caught smuggling rum, you see, and had a very brief trial and was sent off to prison where he could by NO MEANS contact me. Oh, Mother, must we play this awful game?" She put down her cards, rose from her chair and left the room.

CHAPTER 17

An Unexpected Caller

A little while after Grenadine had ended the card game in such an abrupt fashion, Mrs. Fieldpea came to her daughter with a tray of blackberry tea and buttered toast. She found Grenadine dressed for bed, lying across the counterpane, facedown into her pillow. "Tea and toast if it pleases you, dear," Mrs. Fieldpea said, finding, with some complication, a place for the tray on a bedside table crowded with clock and candlestick, diary and pen, books and sundries and pencils in a cup.

Grenadine sat upright on the side of the bed and blew her nose. Twice.

"Mrs. Wickerbench has shown me a very nice stitch, Grenadine," Mrs. Fieldpea said, pouring tea. "Shall I teach it to you?"

"Is it very difficult?" Grenadine asked, wearily.

"Oh, very much to the contrary," her mother said, brightly, "it's remarkably easy, and makes a lovely effect. Shall we take our tray to the sewing room?"

And take it they did. And while Grenadine was getting the hang of the new stitch, Mrs. Fieldpea, at her elbow, said, very softly, "Of course, my dear, things do happen to one, at times—things that are quite beyond one's control."

"I know, Mother," Grenadine said, quietly. She knotted the cotton and bit it off, took a new length from a skein of different color, moistened the end of it in her mouth and, with one eye shut and her tongue between her teeth, threaded the needle and went on. Her mother sipped blackberry tea, ate toast and watched the new stitch take lovely shape in dusty rose and midnight blue before Grenadine rested the embroidery hoop on her lap, looked away and said, sadly, "I've been quite horrid about this, haven't I?"

"You've been badly disappointed, dear," her mother said.

"But if one can't rise above a disappointment, Mother, how is one to be thought a grown-up, after all?" Grenadine said. "And poor Mr. Pickerel. Who knows what really *has* happened to him while I've been thinking only of myself."

"I shouldn't worry about Mr. Pickerel, dear," said her mother. "He strikes me as quite the kind of creature who takes care of him*self*—assiduously."

And, just then, there was a knock at the door. "Mr. Pickerel!" Grenadine said with horror. "And me in my nightdress. Oh, Mother!"

And her mother, whose eyes were almost as wide as Grenadine's at that moment, said, "Well, perhaps it is and perhaps it isn't. We must calm ourselves, and then you must go to your room, dear, while I go to discover who, in fact, *is* knocking at our door at this hour of the evening. All right? Run along, then." And, of course, she did.

Much later that evening Mr. Fieldpea returned from The Tottensea Burrows Midsummer's Night Fancy Dress Cotillion Ball with his two charges, Almandine and Incarnadine, both of them in full flower of fancy dress and brimming over with every excitement which an event of that nature supplies, and, both of them, moreover, almost before they came in the door, saying, as one, "Where's Grenadine!"

"In here, dears," said Grenadine, from the parlor where she and her mother had been waiting patiently, on the lemon yellow damask settee, in night robes and slippers, for the return of the celebrants.

"Grenadine! What has happened?" said Almandine, with great agitation, as the two sisters swept in, crowding the little room with the swish of gowns, the scent of corsages and the flashings of jewelry, with dance programs and pencils and favors and all the trappings of grand events in tow. "Where is Mr. Pickerel? Everyone was looking for you. We were all quite—"

"Grenadine!" Incarnadine breathlessly interrupted her sister. "Merchanty Swift was there! And, you won't believe it, dear. He was asking for you! Merchanty Swift was *there* and he was asking for *you!*"

"Yes," Grenadine said, serenely, "I know."

Almandine and Incarnadine stood up straight and stared at their sister in blank stupefaction. Mr. Fieldpea, who had followed the girls into the room, exchanged some kind of knowing glance with Mrs. Fieldpea, who then said, finally, "Mr. Swift was here, my dears. Earlier this evening."

Almandine and Incarnadine looked at each other, utterly flummoxed, and, after a space, sank to the floor and looked back and forth, now at their mother, now at Grenadine, waiting impatiently for some kind of explanation of this exceptionally puzzling evening.

"Mr. Pickerel never came," Grenadine said, trying to make a start explaining things. "We don't know why." She looked at her sisters and added, weakly, "Mother and I played gin rummy . . . and embroidered . . . and then . . . Mr. Swift came."

"Merchanty Swift came here?" Almandine asked, beyond surprise.

"Right," Grenadine said.

"But . . . ," said Almandine.

"But . . . ," said Incarnadine.

"Mr. Swift was concerned about your sister," Mr. Field-pea said quietly, and the girls turned to look at him.

"How did you know that, Father?" asked Almandine.

"I spoke to him at the ball," Mr. Fieldpea said. "Having just this evening returned from his travels during which he had learned disturbing things about Mr. Pickerel, and also having learned that Mr. Pickerel would be accompanying your sister to the ball, Mr. Swift told me that he had come in the interest of Grenadine's safety. When neither Mr. Pickerel nor Grenadine appeared at the ball, Mr. Swift and I decided that he should come here to be certain that she was safe while I remained at my post, chaperoning you and Incarnadine at the ball."

"But . . . ," said Almandine.

"But . . . ," said Incarnadine.

In the end, the two sisters were more or less satisfied as to the factual particulars of Grenadine's evening, and then, at her request, they set about to impart an unabridged description of all the wonderful things they had experienced at the ball. Following that, they insisted that Grenadine tell them everything, again, leaving out absolutely nothing about Merchanty Swift: How did he act? Was he haughty? Did he talk? What did he say? What did you say, then? When you played at Anagrams, who won? Was he clever at it? Did he take sugar in his tea? How much? Biscuits?

After all that, Almandine said, "Pooh! Your evening was better than ours by twice. I'm jealous."

"And well might you be, dear," said their mother, yawning. "I believe your sister found Mr. Swift's company much to be enjoyed! He's very charming." On her way to bed she turned back to say, "And not a little taken with your sister, I think."

"Mother," Grenadine protested quietly, blushing. But she smiled.

When the girls themselves had finally fallen into beds of exhaustion from both the evening and the talking of it, and when candles were out and good-nights said and the room very quiet, Incarnadine's small tired voice rose out of the darkness: "Did he *let* you win at Anagrams?"

"I believe not," Grenadine said.

*   *   *

And at about that moment, Farnaby Pockets came home to his mother.

"Mother!" he said, breathless and urgent as he came through the door. "Mother!"

"Farnaby!" his mother exclaimed and ran to him.

"Mr. Pickerel!" Farnaby said with a strange wildness in his eyes. "Mr. Pickerel!"

"What about Mr. Pickerel? What's happened, Farnaby?"

CHAPTER 18

What Farnaby Saw by the Rockery

There was a time when some of the field mice used to eat from The Dish of a kindly old creature who had never regarded field mice as anything more than a nuisance. The Dog was totally above malice though not totally above being occasionally cross. Quite often cross, now I think of it. But, in fairness, he was, as I say, old. And I should tell you that many of the mice felt that it was not right to be eating The Dog's food. Discussions were sometimes held over dinner in this matter, and the issue even appeared as an agenda item at the Tottensea Burrows Town Meeting.

"It wasn't meant for us," one side said, respectfully, "it was meant for The Dog."

"Well, actually, if one thinks about it," said the other side, courteously, "the birdseed wasn't meant for us either, being for the birds, you see."

"Yes, I do see what you mean, in a way," said the one side, carefully, so as not to appear argumentative, "but, to take an alternative view, the birdseed was meant for wild creatures, wasn't it? In that sense, one might come to think that we had some claim, being wild creatures ourselves, after all."

"I take your point," said the other side, politely, "but being a 'wild creature,' as you say, hardly makes one a bird, nevertheless, if you see what I'm getting at."

"Yes," said the one side. "Still, in all, there's nothing on the feeder that says 'For birds only' is there? And, beyond that, we only eat the seed that falls to the ground, if you follow my reasoning."

"I do follow that," said the other side, by way of concession, "but what of the vegetable garden, then? *That* certainly was not meant for us."

And here, I'm afraid, there was a long silence, betokening, perhaps, something of a bad conscience among some proportion of the field mice. There were things put forward in reply to this point, but they weren't real arguments. They were things rather more along the line of "But we've always eaten from the vegetable garden" or "Do they really mind us eating from the vegetable garden?" or even "We eat so little, really, when one thinks about it."

"We're not saying that we shouldn't eat from the vegetable garden," said the other side, being very generous in victory, and not at all wanting to embarrass or nonplus one's opponent. "We're only saying that eating from The Dog's Dish is not any different, *in principle,* from eating from the vegetable garden."

At length, Peebles Carryforth The Mayor, thinking, perhaps, that feelings were running a bit high from this spirited discussion, and that time was needed for the matter to find its proper level in the scheme of things, chose not to call a vote and the meeting proceeded to the next item on the agenda. The issue of whether it was quite right to eat from The Dish, therefore, remained an ethical gray area until it was abruptly resolved for the mice in a way no one expected. For, receiving no clear guidance from the Town Meeting *not* to eat from The Dish, many mice continued *to* eat from The Dish—and that quite often. Finally, though, as might have been feared, one of them ate from The Dish and was not properly cautious about it.

Though The Woman had remarked to The Man that The Dog had been eating rather awfully well lately, neither of them, for the longest time, saw an actual mouse. But late one afternoon, when the sun had almost, but *not quite,* finished going down for the day, little Harrington Doubletooth ascended to The Dish. And when he sat, for some moments, very unwisely, eating The Dog's rations in that remaining bit of daylight—small as it was—The Woman SAW him!

"Shoo!" The Woman said from the window. "SHOO!" she said again, very loud, and then she made an alarming thunderclap with her hands. Poor little unthinking Harrington Doubletooth ran right down the nearest hole, covered his ears, closed his eyes and resolved never again to eat from any dog dish anywhere in the world whether in daylight or darkness of night for as long as he did live! But at that point it hardly mattered what he resolved to do or not to do. For inside The Cottage The Woman was talking to The Man at that very moment—and about Harrington Doubletooth, too! And, after that discussion, EVENTS were set into motion.

*   *   *

It was a few days after Harrington Doubletooth's mistake that Farnaby Pockets had seen Mr. Pickerel come out of The Brambles and had seen the Saracen dagger hanging from his patent leather belt. He determined to have a look at it, Farnaby did. But by the time he had shinned down the rhododendron, Mr. Pickerel was right out of sight. So he went after him, overtaking him just beyond the rockery. And exactly when Farnaby was about to hail him, a great yellow something fell upon Mr. Pickerel.

Mr. Langston Pickerel, terror of some of the smaller sea-lanes of the world and onetime leader of certain unsavory characters whom hardly anyone enjoyed spending time with, Mr. Langston Pickerel, swordsanimal extraordinaire who, being much on his dignity, was not to be trifled with by other small creatures, Mr. Langston Pickerel, genteel and chivalrous courtier of many fair damsels in a number of exotic venues and flawless quoter of Byron, Shelley, Keats, Wordsworth, Walter de la Mare and a few others I'd never heard of, Mr. Langston Pickerel, petite lion of strange fashions, connoisseur, raconteur, animal about town and a whole host of other things, was, among them, NOT a match for a Large Yellowish Stripy Cat. Not even close.

"Formi*dable!*" Pickerel had time to say, in French, on looking up and seeing The Cat, in midair, above him. And that was all. His rapier, we are told, never cleared the sheath.

Farnaby Pockets saw it happen—a frightening spasm of violence right in front of him. Furious and rough it was and all of it well within The Cat's control. And when The Cat's teeth sank into the back of its victim's neck, poor Mr. Pickerel shuddered and went slack. The Cat dropped him onto the ground and stood up over him in triumph. Bristling and awful The Cat was, Farnaby thought—and strangely motionless but for the rolling arabesques along its great yellow tail.

Farnaby dove into the rockery. He pressed himself deep into crannies of the rocks and stayed there, trembling, for a very long time. After darkness had come and the trembling had passed a little, Farnaby began to think what he was going to do. He devised a route in his mind. From the rockery he would make straight for the porpoise fountain, he decided. Yes. There would be safety under the fountain. And the stone-flagged terrace was close by that. There were tunnels under the flags. Beyond the terrace were the garden urns— four of them—with very short exposure between them. . . .

Good as the plan seemed, it was very late before he got up the nerve to actually stick his nose out of the rockery. It was later still when that nerve was enough to send him dashing out across open ground toward the porpoise fountain. There was a pounding in his ears and he thought his heart might burst, but he made it. He waited under the fountain, panting and thinking of his next move. Then out he went and ran for the flags.

So he found his wit and his courage that strange midsummer's night and, with only those to bear him up in his peril, young Farnaby Pockets, in such a way, took himself safely home by degrees.

151

CHAPTER 19

The Turning of the Wheel

Opportune Baggs was a light sleeper. Octavia Baggs was well home from the Cotillion Ball and asleep beside him when he woke up disappointed with the Mousewriter. The flourishes were not right to his way of thinking, nor the curlicues, either, for that matter. Rather too stiff, both of them. He lay in the darkness, thinking and thinking. Then, abruptly, he went bolt upright in the bed and knew what he wanted to do about it. Up and into his slippers. Robed over his nightshirt, he lit a candle and took it to the workshop.

The solution might be in the flourisher adjustment wheel, he thought, and nothing more than that. So he turned it—turned the flourisher adjustment wheel right round from *Flexible More or Less,* clean past *Rather Flexible* and all the way to *Ever So Flexible.* "There," he said to himself. And he tried it.

He rejoiced. The curlicues were now exactly as he wanted them. And the flourishes! Easy, flowing and graceful—the flourishes warmed his heart. "Now," he said to himself. "Now for a real sentence. Real words." But it wasn't to be. Not on that night, at least. Many nights would come and go before he would make another curlicue, even—let alone a real sentence made of words. For someone was knocking on his front door, insistently, and over and over. He would go to answer it. And after he answered it nothing would ever be the same for Opportune Baggs again. Or for any other Baggs. Or for any mouse in Tottensea.

It was a long and winding way up from the workshop to the Baggses' front door. "Who on earth would knock and knock and just keep *on* knocking at this hour?" he asked himself. Though merely perplexed at first, in the end he was almost peeved about so much unabated knocking. He pulled the door open roughly, as if to say, "What!"

Merchanty Swift was standing on his doorstep and with a darker look on him than Opportune Baggs had ever seen on that normally bright countenance. "Tottensea Hall in half an hour," Swift said. "We have a cat, it seems."

This, and happenings like it, would take place all over Tottensea Burrows because, a little earlier, a brave Mrs. Pockets, with her mouseling, had gone through that dangerous night to wake the Mayor and tell him what Farnaby saw. "Come in, please," the Mayor had said to them, in a voice still thick with sleep. "I was afraid of this. Give me a moment, if you will," and he went off to dress himself. He returned to them, resolute and full of grim energy. "I must be gone for a little while. Will you wait?" They agreed to it and he went off to wake the General.

Clementine Nickelpenny was normally a very good sleeper. But she had been unaccountably awake that night and, as she lay there, her mind casting about, she thought about *Milli-*

cent's Surprised Heart and how very happy it was at the end with Major Willowbrook. And she thought about the only military mouse she knew and how much she wished he would pay more attention to a few practical civilian things. "Things like *love* for goodness' sakes!" she said, and said it actually out loud. And because it *was* out loud, she turned as red-faced there, alone, in her bed, as a mouse ever gets. And, perhaps thinking the dark of night insufficient, by itself, to hide such a high coloring, she pulled the covers over her head, as well.

There was a knocking. It startled her, and, as she was well awake, she went immediately and opened the door. There, on the front stoop, standing right in front of her, was General Random Chewings! Talk about your surprised hearts.

The General had his mouth all formed up to say something to Merchanty Swift about The Cat. He was somehow completely unprepared to see Clementine Nickelpenny before him there—and looking so beautiful, at that, in her uncommonly rosy complexion, he thought. For a long moment, cat or no cat, he just did stand there.

"General Chewings!" Mrs. Nickelpenny said, finally, out of her own surprise.

"Yes, well," the General recovered and cleared his throat with awkwardness. "I must talk to Swift, you see. There's a cat, isn't there?"

"Oh my word!" she said, with real alarm. "Come in, please, General. I'll wake him at once."

Swift appeared quickly, buckling his belt as he came. He and the General spoke briefly in the hallway, went out the door together and off to their respective missions—Chewings to the Fieldpeas, Swift to the Baggses. Fieldpeas and Baggses would go on to warn others. And so, as if the River Stith, itself, shot its banks and poured remorseless down into every nook and hole of Tottensea, news of The Cat rushed through their tunnels and brought the field mice up—turned them out of their pleasant homes as surely as any torrent would of black waters in the night.

Tottensea Hall, late scene of such merriment and happiness, became, that night, a place of anguish. The garlands hung from its chandeliers still, but hung limp, as if weeping at the passing of something, as if the room itself were knowing that it never would again share the joys of these harmless little creatures huddling now against its walls. Not in flowing gowns they were and dignified tunics, but in whatever clothes they threw on in the night. Not laughing and happy and dancing they were, but hollow-eyed and afraid.

The Mayor stood at the front of the hall with Farnaby and Mrs. Pockets beside him, waiting for Tottensea. When he thought they had all gathered—or when he dared not wait a moment longer—he asked Farnaby if he would tell what he had seen. But as the young mouse was much too nervous to do anything of the sort, the Mayor, himself, told the story of Langston Pickerel's demise as best he could and asked Farnaby if he had got it right.

"Yes sir. It was just like that," Farnaby said, in a very small voice. "Only quicker."

The room of mice trembled as one.

The discussion was urgent and compelling. What were they to do? Some spoke with feeling of the life they had built in the burrows, of their fondness for the old places and the old ways, and of their fear of the new and the unknown. Must they really leave their homes? Would another place be any safer? What was OUT THERE, away from The Cottage: they wondered aloud. What things worse than cats, perhaps?

"Nothing is worse than cats!" answered others of them.

"But cats do not swoop onto you from the sky! Nor tunnel after you in your dens!"

"But can we live *here,* exactly where the cat will spend all his days?"

Merchanty Swift came to the front. "Dear ones," he said, "we are in terrible distress, here, and I am loath to add to the burden of that distress—but so I must. There are two in our midst who may speak with awful authority on this matter of cats. I beg them to speak, now, and I beg you to listen."

Haltingly, and with shaking in their voices, Mrs. Nickelpenny and Mrs. Pockets, each in turn, rose and told a terrifying tale. As the mice listened to the fate of Sweetcream Burrows, fear rose from their midst like smoke, then encompassed them like flames. Tottensea was trapped in terror and indecision. What must they do? What?

It was just here, then, that the humble leadership of Peebles Carryforth The Mayor came into play. He was respected and regarded. But he was a quiet mouse, only willing to help when he was wanted. As the debate had gone on, some mice had begun to look at him. What did he think? He was, after all, their leader. Then others had looked at him. And when they heard about Sweetcream Burrows they all looked at him! They hungered for his thoughts, for his sense, for decision! It was only then that he thought it his duty to speak.

There are times when strength falls away, when speed and

cleverness, even, will not suffice. There are times when nothing will do but wisdom. This was that time, and he, Peebles Carryforth The Mayor, must give them that wisdom.

"My friends," he said, quietly and earnestly, "The Cat is a terrible enemy, it is true, with much skill and cunning to hunt us down—whether by ones or by twos. But it is not, after all, The Cat that we are faced with. It is something much worse." The mice looked at one another, puzzled and not comforted.

"What we are faced with," continued the Mayor, "is THE WRATH OF THE OWNERS. It is The Man and The Woman who brought The Cat here. But if The Cat fails in his terrible purpose, that will not be the end of this matter. No, indeed! You may count upon it that there will be other measures—traps and poisons, probably."

The mice drew sharp breaths at such a thought.

"The Man, The Woman—this place that we are living in belongs to them," the Mayor said, dispassionately. "Be very sure that they will have their way here. It is we, dear friends, who are out of place. We are field mice, after all. And it is to the fields that we must return. The fields! The hedgerows! They are the fixed regions of our intended ways. We must search them out: the spaces we are to inhabit, the foods meant for us, there, and the natural covers and protections provided for us. My friends, the appointed place of our lives is abroad before us! Let us make this peril into great benefit. May it drive us to our rightful station. In all urgency I say to you that we must go out."

He looked around at them all. And then he said it again, almost in a whisper: "We must go out."

There was no further debate. After the vote, the decision being what it was, they all wept together for a little. But events were overtaking them and they must get hold of themselves. There was hardly time for weeping! And none at all for consoling! "That must come later, dear," they said to one another, as bravely as they could. "We must pluck up, now, and pack our things!" And off they went. But . . . all pluck aside, the tears *would* come, wouldn't they?

CHAPTER 20

*Tottensea, Bag
and Baggage*

Mrs. Pockets and Farnaby, when they thought about their boardinghouse and all the things they owned, realized, of course, that they couldn't take the furniture as it was much too heavy to carry, and they couldn't carry all the kitchen utensils, as there were too many of them. So Mrs. Proserpine Pockets said, firmly and with hardly a tear, that they must take only a few of their most precious possessions, and not too many of those, either, for they would certainly have to carry some things for poor old Miss Middlechippers, if, indeed, they did not have to carry poor old Miss Middlechippers, herself!

In the middle of the night, then, they both filled pillowcases with their most precious things. Mrs. Pockets put into her pillowcase the little framed portrait of Mr. Pockets along with the chiming clock from the parlor, some of her best silver, two practical dresses and a pale yellow table scarf which had been embroidered with blue forget-me-nots by her greataunt Salisaw Halfcott long before she was born. Farnaby put Mr. Feet, his stuffed caterpillar, into his pillowcase along with a toy wheelbarrow, some clothes which his mother said were practical and the rock which he had found that looked like a frog on one side and like a rock on the other.

Farnaby asked his mother about their secret hiding place and the little sock that held their hard-earned savings and his mother replied, as cheerfully as she could at that time of night and under those very trying circumstances, that, alas, she was afraid the little sock that held their hard-earned savings was quite empty because of all the money that they were owed by Mr. Neversmythe. Then Mrs. Pockets looked at Farnaby as if she had just thought of something important and said, "Mr. Neversmythe's locker!"

On their way to Mr. Neversmythe's room, Mrs. Pockets said that if there was any money in the locker they must take only enough to pay for what Mr. Neversmythe owed them and not a mousefarthing more.

"But how shall we open it?" Farnaby said. "Mr. Neversmythe always wears the key around his neck."

"Hmm," Mrs. Pockets said. "Yes, that's true, isn't it? Well, we must try to open it anyway. Perhaps he has hidden another key in the room somewhere."

But although they searched in the dresser drawers, on top of the wardrobe, under the mattress and everywhere else they could think of, they could not find another key. The locker was quite locked, all right, and looked sturdy. Mrs. Pockets said, "Well, my dear, we must try banging on it, I think." And they did. But while the lock did not break open as they had hoped, something else did happen. When Farnaby struck the lock with the doorstop, the locker itself moved. Now Mrs. Pockets and Farnaby had thought that if the locker was full of money, as they hoped, it should be very heavy. But they now discovered that it wasn't heavy at all. In fact, when they lifted it, it seemed possible that it was completely empty. Their hearts sank a little as they felt quite sure they would get nothing of value from the locker to collect Mr. Neversmythe's debt. "Let's carry it into the kitchen," Mrs. Pockets said as she took the handle on one end and Farnaby took the one on the other. "Perhaps we can open it with a utensil of some sort." But before he had gone two steps down the stairs, Farnaby accidentally dropped his end and the locker tumbled and bumped and crashed all the way to the bottom and landed upside down and open!

Just as Mrs. Pockets and Farnaby suspected, there was almost nothing in it. Only a single piece of paper had fallen out of the locker and lay on the floor beneath it. Scrawled on the paper, in very poor penmanship, was the following:

Neversmythe,

Knowing full well what it is you thought was in this footlocker, it gives me a peculiar kind of pleasure to inform you that what you hoped was in here ain't. We got it.

And I don't mind telling you that if it was any good to us we wouldn't be communicating with the likes of you. But the fact is, Neversmythe, this blasted map ain't no good to nobody because the booty's already been dug up. Our old friend has double-crossed us again.

All we know for sure is that he disappeared after that raid in which you, sir, like to have got us all killed. It's very plain he wanted us to think that he was killed but we don't. But then he ain't living among no voles we can find neither. So we think he's hidin' out with some other kind of crea-

tures in one of his fancy disguises. But since he can't resist showin' off that jeweled dagger we'll find him sooner or later.

We have voted and what we say is this: despise you as we may, if you find him before we do, we'll cut you in for a full share of anything we can get out of him. If you do find him let us know. He ain't no match for all of us at once.

Yours etc.,

Scratcher Doheeny

"What does it mean?" Farnaby asked his mother.

"It means that Mr. Pickerel was not a field mouse. Now, Farnaby, while I finish up here, please run next door and see how Miss Middlechippers fares. Help her with her things, dear, and bring her back with you. Then we must go to join the others. Quickly, now. It gets very late."

Farnaby hurried right out the door and smack into someone—someone strong and grown-up, someone he had seen before, someone who, once again, took hold of him with an iron grip and who had a gold ring in his ear and a patch over one eye.

As for the Fieldpeas, I must tell you that they were discouraged beyond measure. They had to make difficult choices about which personal things were most dear to them, yes. But it wasn't that. In that, they were no worse off, nor better, than anyone in Tottensea Burrows. No, they weren't feeling sorry for themselves on that account.

It was the bookshop.

They gathered there, the five of them, and stood in desolation, looking helplessly at hundreds of books. Hundreds of them, I tell you! Of course, you know what they were thinking. "How many books can a mouse carry?" is what they were thinking. "There are five of us. And all these books!"

One or two of the girls broke down, briefly, and sobbed, I'm afraid. But we must try to remember how tired they had been when they fell into bed that night. And here they were, barely an hour or two later, facing an impossible task like this and where would they sleep the next night and nothing would ever be the same for them again and who could tell them how all this would end and . . . would you just *look* at all those books!

There was a small knocking on the door of The Bookish Mouse. Wearily, but still with some curiosity, too, Mrs. Emmalina Fieldpea went to the door and opened it. And there before her, of all things, stood the Fidgetsons! All seven*teen* of them! What were they doing here? There was Mr. Fidgetson and Mrs. Fidgetson and behind the two of them, peeking round skirt and trousers of their parents, were all manner of little Fidgetsons.

Mr. Fidgetson said, "We were thinking you might need help with the books."

Letitia Fidgetson took two of them—mouseling books, hers were, and so beautifully illustrated that she wished she could sit down with them, right there. Thurgood Fidgetson, completely on the other hand, was alto*gether* pleased that he would not have to read his book, now or at any other time, because he had looked through it twice and there were no pictures. Not a single one. Still, it was the book Grenadine Fieldpea had handed him and he would do his duty by it.

"This is a wonderful poetry book, Thurgood," Grenadine had said to him. "I hope you'll be very careful with it." And, of course, Thurgood *was* careful—famously careful, as it turned out. In fact, to this day, no one has any idea how he ever managed to *be* so careful with that book!

The Fidgetsons' help was heartening, of course, though hardly a solution to the problem. But no sooner had the Fidgetsons gone off with twenty-six books in cartage (by Incarnadine's reckoning) than in trooped the Chiselteeths! And there were *nine*teen of *them* (three full litters!). And the Baileywiks came after that. Fifteen of *them*. And the Fusibles. Nine, I believe. Fourteen Scatterbys. Ten Gnawlings. Twelve Cheddarlees. And I lost count. You could ask Incarnadine how many families came to carry off books that night. Incarnadine would know.

Emmalina Fieldpea absolutely teared up when she realized how much these mice loved books. And she was glad for every oat-seed cake and every dollop of blackthorn jam that she had ever served up to these wonderful friends at four o'clock of an afternoon. It had been well worth it, she said to Almandine, who was standing on a ladder handing books down to her (which she, in turn, handed on to Glendowner and Grenadine, who were making the decisions while Incarnadine kept the count). It had been more than just worth it, Emmalina said, on second thought. It had been a high privilege.

Certainly, they didn't get all the books out that night. Its shelves were far from empty when The Bookish Mouse closed for the last time. But thanks to the kindness and thoughtfulness of many friends and to the general love of books all round Tottensea, most of the great mouseclassics were saved.

*   *   *

There were no tears at the Baggs place on the night of leaving Tottensea Burrows, as the whole family was entirely too busy trying to save the Mousewriter. Since Opportune Baggs couldn't think of leaving his machine behind and since it was altogether too big and complicated to carry with them as it was, he did the only reasonable thing. He and some of the children took it apart and parceled it out to various members of the family, piece by piece.

This meant that Parnassus Baggs, for example, not only sorted through his own things, that evening, to choose his favorite books, toys, clothes and drawings to take along, but that he also occupied himself with loosening the three upper set screws on the frontmost jack pawl cleat located just below the right knee treadle linkage so that he could then disengage the rear toggle pin from the longitudinal coupling strap. This, of course, freed up the transverse wedging latchet very nicely so that it could be carried off into the night by, say, Andronicus Baggs, along with his cricket bat, a pair of ice skates and one or two peanut butter sandwiches.

Merchanty Swift told Mrs. Nickelpenny to take only her own things that night. "Don't trouble for any of this," he said, dismissing his considerable possessions with a careless wave of his paw. "It's only stuff, after all, and the world's full of it." Nevertheless, he *did* sling a small satchel over his shoulder that night—a satchel into which he had packed certain pewter tankards (and packed them carefully, I might add, to forestall any clanking about as he walked). But they were all he took, those tankards. And only those for love of his friends.

Sir Rotherham took the silver tea service that had been in

the Twickets family from as far back as the mice had any history of. Umpteen Weeks went with his walking cane and said he wouldn't need any of the other nonsense. The General of Tottensea Burrows packed the Clausewitz and a handsome brace of flintlock pistols he'd bought off an Etruscan shrew who had decided to stick to teeth, he said.

Quicklesmith Peets carried pickling jars away that night. And Wrinkles Freestone took a rocking chair.

So it went throughout Tottensea Burrows. All under the ground, many different kinds of bags and trunks and suitcases were sternly tested through a long and difficult night as everyone thought of just one more thing that must be stuffed into them if at all possible. And after a night of bewildering decisions and many questions (such as "But, Mother, may I have my toys again when we come back?") and while comforting pats were being administered all round, the burrows of Tottensea were finally, and most reluctantly, boarded up. And, in the small hours of a summer morning, a long thin column of heavyhearted and overladen little emigrants streamed out across a moonlit lawn in search of security and better prospects for the children—prospects such as growing up, for example.

CHAPTER 21

Bad Animals

When Farnaby Pockets had run out the door to fetch Miss Middlechippers and had run right into Mr. Frenchie Grimwott and had made a sound like "Oof!" in doing it, Mrs. Pockets heard the small commotion and went toward the door. But then she backed away from that door as through it came a most alarming collection of creatures, all of them dressed in rough clothing and hatted with strange headwear—tricorns, spotted kerchiefs and a wide-brimmed thing or two with feathers on them. She saw that each of them carried a weapon of some kind on his hip or stuffed into his belt. "Bandits!" she thought to herself. "Or pirates, more like!" They came crowding into her little kitchen, as many as could do, until it was quite overrun. There was a vole, several lemmings and some ship rats in her kitchen and more outside, looking in the door. One of the lemmings she knew. And her heart jumped as she saw that a large bad-looking ship rat was holding on to Farnaby.

The vole stepped forward a little, removed his three-cornered hat and held it, respectfully, as it were, with both paws, in front of his chest. "Don't be alarmed, mum," he said.

Mrs. Proserpine Pockets was *very* alarmed. "Who are you?" she said. "What do you want? Give me my boy!"

None of the brigands moved. The vole cleared his throat and spoke, formally, as if he had prepared a speech, "I am Mr. Doheeny, at your service, mum." He dipped his head slightly in a small and, under the circumstances, entirely ridiculous gesture of courtesy and he grinned at her in a leering sort of way that made the skin on the back of her neck feel as if it were trying to crawl away and hide in some other place.

"And it has come to our attention," Mr. Doheeny went on, "through the good offices of our dear friend Mr. Neversmythe, here, who I understand took lodgings in this very place, that you may be in position to be of wondrous help to the poor humble creatures as you see before you now." He turned his hat in his paws as he talked. "We be interested to find the abode of a certain departed animal who by great villainy has tooken to himself much worldly goods what was owed to us by right. And if you'll only be so kind, now, mum, as to direct us to that abode, then we'll be on our way, and leavin' you with our unbounded gratitude for your most creaturely kindness!"

"What animal?" Mrs. Pockets said.

"Aye. And there's the rub, then, ain't it? Us not bein' party to what name it is you know him by, mum—him bein' in disguise and all and not his proper self, shockin' as it seems. But he'll be that self-same animal who came into this very place and frightened off poor Mr. Neversmythe, here, who never had done him no harm as long as he did live, mum, and did that frightenin', too, right before your very own eyes, as I'm told."

"Mr. Pickerel, you mean," Mrs. Pockets said.

"Aye. Who's that you say? 'Pickerel' is it? Now *there's* a name for you, lads! 'Mr. Pickerel' he called hisself in these parts. Well, ain't that a tidy moniker, then. I'll be thankin' you, mum, for clearin' up that bit o' mystery." And some of his crew snickered and said the name "Pickerel!" to one another in an unpleasant manner. The vole snickered too, but then he got very serious, his eyes narrowed into something like a scowl and he said, in a different tone of voice and more quietly. "And where did this . . . Mr. Pickerel keep hisself and his things, if you please, mum?"

"Give me my boy, first," said Mrs. Pockets.

The vole edged closer. Mrs. Pockets would have moved back to keep a distance, but as she was already against a wall, she could only move her head to one side to let the vole know that he was too close. But, indeed, it was all the vole's purpose to be too close.

"Just tell us what you know, then," the vole said, calmly, in a sort of growl. And, looking right into her eyes, he added, slowly, "If you please, mum."

"He . . . He sometimes stayed at the pub, I believe," Mrs. Pockets said in a frightened and unsteady voice.

"The pub!" The vole's eyes brightened as he said it. "Yes, of course, the pub—The Silver . . . The Silver . . ."

"Claw," said Mr. Neversmythe, who had come to the front of the group and now stood beside the vole. Mr. Neversmythe's eyes met the eyes of Mrs. Pockets for a moment. The bog lemming looked away.

"The Silver Claw, yes," the vole repeated. And then his manner changed again. He was all business, suddenly.

"We'll take your boy with us as a kind of . . . guarantee, so to speak. If all is as you say, then we'll send him back to you straightaway—safe and sound as ever you please." He made to go and the room cleared quickly. The vole turned back to close the door and said, "For your boy's sake, then, mum, you'll be stayin' here, won't you, until we send him back to you, all safe and sound, as I say." His awful grin came back, suddenly. He gave a little bow and then closed the door, quietly, leaving poor Mrs. Pockets alone with her worst fears.

Although it seemed like hours to Mrs. Pockets, it was, actually, only a little while later that someone knocked on her door. When she opened it, there, before her, to her great joy, stood Mr. Merchanty Swift Who Brought The Cheese Trade Down To Earth Almost Single-Handedly. And as soon as she saw him, Mrs. Pockets burst into tears.

The Brambles was at the far edge of Tottensea Burrows. Merchanty Swift often went out there to see after the Pock-etses and to make sure they were all right. He would bring them things: food or clothing, a toy for Farnaby, furniture for the boardinghouse—whatever he thought they might need. And on this night when all Tottensea packed up their things, he thought he'd better see to them, as well.

"Whatever is wrong, my dear?" he said, putting his arms around Mrs. Pockets to comfort her as she wept.

"They've . . . they've taken Farnaby," said Mrs. Pockets trying her very best to speak clearly between sobs.

"Who? Who's taken Farnaby?" said Merchanty Swift as he stood away from her, indignant at the very idea of someone taking Farnaby Pockets away from his mother.

"Ruffians!" she said, still between her sobs. "Bad animals. Very bad, I think."

"When?"

"A little while ago."

"Do you know where they've taken him, dear?"

"I think so," Mrs. Pockets said, not sobbing quite so much, now. She wiped her eyes with the little handkerchief that she kept in her apron pocket and said, "I believe they've taken him . . . to The Silver Claw." And then she wiped her eyes again.

"The Silver Claw? And do you know why they've taken him *there*?"

"Yes," she said, feeling hopeful, for some reason, now that Merchanty Swift was there and asking questions. "I believe I do. They're looking for Mr. Pickerel's things, they said."

Merchanty Swift looked at the floor for a bit. He touched his mouth with a paw and said, "Yes. Well, they think he kept treasure there, you see." He looked at the floor some more. He was thinking. At last he said, "Very well. The Silver Claw, then. I'll go there at once." He took Mrs. Pockets' paw in his own and said, "Please try not to worry, dear Mrs. Pockets. Farnaby is very brave. He'll be all right, I think. I will see about this." And he left her.

CHAPTER 22

How Merchanty Swift
Did Business with Pirates

Merchanty Swift hurried himself directly to The Silver Claw. He found a door that had been forced open and went inside. The place was dark but he could hear voices. As he was making his way, carefully, across the pub's main room, dodging tables and chairs in the darkness as he went, he was startled by a voice somewhere behind him. "Stop where ye be, laddie," the voice said in a low and threatening tone. Merchanty Swift stood quite still. And then, very loud, the voice cried out, "In here, mates!"

Into the room, then, through two or three different doors came ship rats and lemmings, several of them carrying lanterns. Last of all came a vole, holding on to Farnaby.

"Well, who'll this be, then?" said Scratcher Doheeny. He let go of Farnaby Pockets and drew his cutlass. "State your business, stranger."

"I'm not armed," Swift said. "I've come for the boy."

"Have you, then? You hear that, lads? He's come for the boy, he has. And why should we take any notice of *what* the likes of you has come for, mouse?"

175

"Because you're after treasure, I think," Swift said, cool as you please, "and there's none here. Am I right?"

"Could be. So?"

"The boy can't help you with that. I can."

"And who might you be, then, that you can show us where the scoundrel hid our treasure."

"Not that treasure. That treasure doesn't exist anymore. Pickerel spent it all on those ridiculous clothes."

"And how would you know that, then?"

"I sold him most of them."

The vole thought about this for a moment. He looked at Swift, doubtfully. "And where did you get clothes like that?"

"It's my business," Swift said. He looked at the vole steadily. "Creatures want something. I get it for them." The vole squinted at him, suspiciously, as if he thought he was being outsmarted or tricked, and he didn't like it. "What kind of treasure do you want?" Swift asked straightforwardly, doing business.

"Eh? What kind of question is that, then? Gold, of course!" The other animals grunted their approval and nodded to one another. "Gems," the vole said. "Ready wealth. You try my patience, mouse. What do you know?"

"I know a lot, friend. But let the boy go, first."

It got very quiet. Scratcher Doheeny looked at Merchanty Swift for a long minute. He looked around at his crew. He looked at the ceiling. He chewed his lip. He looked back at Swift. "All right. You for him, then. But if you lie, mouse, you pays for it with your own blood."

There was a general agreement about this. The crew growled, "That's it, then," and "He's got it right, he does" and

"Your own blood, vermin!" and things like that. And some of them drew knives and fingered the blades of them.

Swift called Farnaby to him, knelt down and spoke quietly, "Go to your mother. Tell her to go and join the others and, Farnaby, listen to me: tell your mother not to send anyone here to try to help me. They won't be able to help me and they'll die for trying. That's very important. Do you understand?"

Farnaby nodded vigorously.

"There's a good lad," Swift said and he winked at him. He leaned and whispered into his ear, "I think we'll see each other again. Now go."

And Farnaby went right out of The Silver Claw and into the night. Then he ran and ran.

So it was that The Brambles door opened yet again that night, bursting open this time, to let in Farnaby—much out of breath but returned to his mother as safe and sound as ever she could have wished but with no thanks whatever to Mr. Scratcher Doheeny.

"My dear!" said Mrs. Pockets, running to her boy. She went to him and kissed him and held him to herself as tightly as it was safe to do, quite overtaken with all the relief and happiness that a little mouse's mother could hold at a moment like that!

"What has happened?" she said, her tears flowing from relief and happiness, but from anxiety, as well. "What of Mr. Swift?"

"He traded himself for me, Mother!" Farnaby said, his eyes very wide.

"Dear Mr. Swift!" Mrs. Pockets said, and held her handkerchief to her eyes.

"The bad creatures were very angry with me, Mother."

"But why, darling? You hadn't done anything!"

"They thought there would be treasure there. In Mr. Pickerel's rooms. But there wasn't any treasure. There was only the clothing. Lots and lots of clothing! They tore it all to pieces, looking for blasted doubloons. What are blasted doubloons, Mother?"

"It's a kind of money, my love."

"They didn't find *any* blasted doubloons, Mother. Not a single one. And they were so angry about that. They all looked at me."

"Oh, my dear!" Mrs. Pockets said and pulled Farnaby close against her.

Farnaby felt very safe there, snuggled against his mother. He said, "Mr. Pickerel had very strange clothes, Mother."

"I know," she said, quietly.

Farnaby pulled away a little so that he could look up at his mother's face. She saw that he was troubled. "Some of Mr. Pickerel's clothes were made from the skin of some poor animal, Mother. From its fur!"

"Yes, I know," she said, and pulled his face back against her. She stroked him, gently. "Try not to think about it, love," she said.

"I thought they were going to do something to me," Farnaby said, his voice muffled against his mother's apron. "They were so angry." He pulled his face away again. "But then Mr. Swift came! And he traded himself for me, Mother! He said we were to go and join the others. And he said it was very important that we not send anyone to try to help him. He said they wouldn't be able to help him and that they would die. And then I ran all the way home."

Farnaby and his mother looked at one another. Then Farnaby said, in a whisper, as if he were afraid to say it out loud, "What will happen to him, Mother?"

"I don't know, darling," Mrs. Pockets said, speaking barely above a whisper, herself. "Mr. Swift is very clever. I think we must do as he says." And she pulled Farnaby to her, again.

"I ran all the way," Farnaby said into his mother's apron. She stroked his head and they held each other close for a little while, saying nothing at all.

After that, then, they collected Miss Middlechippers and hurried off to join the others.

CHAPTER 23

The Hesitation at Lawn's End

The Cottage was located in, as we say, the country. And when the mice came to the actual end of The Cottage's lawn they experienced what I think we shall have to call a hesitation.

It is here, therefore, that we must pause to consider how these particular mice had lived for some time from the largesse of The Cottage and from such of its comforts as The Bird Feeder, The Vegetable Garden, The Compost Heap and lately, unhappily, of course, The Dish. So when the leaders of the little migration stopped at the lawn's end to consider what it was they were to do and where it was they were to go, we must try not to be harsh. We cannot deny, of course, that the entire company had become somewhat soft and, yes, even complacent in their easy life of convenient foraging in the environs of The Cottage. I, myself, would not actually argue against the conclusion that they had become, as we moderns say, spoilt. But the charge, as some have made, that they were hardly *field* mice at all by then—well, I think that goes a deal too far. But they were soft. Yes. I give you soft.

However that may be, it was exactly here, in the order of things, that Sir Rotherham stepped forward to give remarks.

SIR ROTHERHAM'S ADDRESS AT LAWN'S END
While not wishing to . . . and so forth and so on, I would beg your indulgence for a very few moments, and so on. [Breath.] Being in some difficulty, here, and so forth, we find ourselves called upon . . . ah . . . to rise and so forth to great, umm, ah . . . to rise to great . . . umm . . . things . . . and so forth. Yes. Thank you very much. Umm. [Breath. Warm applause.]

Whether "heartened" may perhaps be too strong a word for the effect upon the company of Sir Rotherham's speech, I leave for others to report. What I can tell you is how relieved they all were that the old mouse remained upright—which thing, in all honesty, probably accounted for the applause more than anything he said. It was always so distressing to them when he fell down from not breathing properly during a speech.

After the address, it fell to General Random Chewings, thereupon, to summon a meeting of the Prudence Committee. And, as I can assure you, if any mouse had been under illusions about the seriousness of their situation he would have been brought to his senses by nothing more than the convening of this body. Field mice simply don't do this sort of thing without the most serious provocation. They are not bureaucratic. It's one of their most likable qualities.

There gathered, then, under a clear moon and in the shelter of a lovely little border of sweet alyssum, five good field mice: General Chewings himself, Peebles Carryforth The Mayor, Mr. Glendowner Fieldpea, Opportune Baggs The Inventor, and, of course, Sir Rotherham. Thus assembled, The Committee—as was their habit—considered the business before them with gravity and dispatch. They began with tea.

While Sir Rotherham poured, the General summarized their position as perhaps only a military mouse might have done. "We are faced," he said, "with what appears to be a tolerably steep decline beginning at the edge of the lawn and tending somewhat downward. Thank you, Sir Rotherham . . . just the sugar please. Oh. And one of those. And as said decline could, possibly, be bounded on its nether edge by a blockage of some sort—some impediment to convenient passage, shall we say—the question before this committee is, I believe, should we make to travel—with all our sundries and baggage—right down this difficult and sloping terrain, straightaway, from whence it might be most arduous to recover, or, alternatively, should we send out a scouting party to appraise the prospects. I'll have just one more of those cheeses if it wouldn't be inconvenient, Sir Rotherham."

Sir Rotherham, brandishing the silver teapot with a certain flair, said that since time was of the essence and since there was duty to be lived up to, after all, and since glory was never to be cheaply won and since one must be prepared for the worst while keeping a keen eye out for opportunities, of course—what ho! After this small speech, then, he gave the General his cheese.

As was sometimes true of Sir Rotherham's speeches, they

all thought this one brave, to be sure, spirited, certainly, inspiring in its own way, yes, but, in the end, as a call to action, it was, if one thought about it, vague.

Peebles Carryforth The Mayor said that Merchanty Swift would certainly know what was at the bottom of that slope. They all agreed with this and sent someone off to find him. But Merchanty Swift was not to be found. Not just then, anyway. Indeed, he was very busy elsewhere. Dangerously busy.

Merchanty Swift was, in fact, at that very moment taking the pirates on a tour of his warehouses. Although there were no doubloons there, he told them—and very little gold of any kind, actually—there were lots of other things they might have a look at. They frowned about there not being any doubloons or much gold of any kind and grumped and growled and were very displeased. Their mood became increasingly dangerous as Swift steered the tour in certain directions, showing them all kinds of things he was quite sure they wouldn't be interested in until, finally—to his great relief—one of them said, "What's in them crates in the corner, there?"

"Oh, let's not bother with those," Merchanty Swift said.

"Eh?"

"But over here, now, is a wonderful assortment of Spanish lace you might want to see. Very nice workmanship, in my opinion."

"Hang the lace, vermin! What's in the crates?"

"Never mind that," Swift said. "Here! Do you like plaid?"

Within moments, of course, the crates in the corner were well torn apart, the bottles opened and the wine being lavishly guzzled with all manner of shocking greediness! Merchanty Swift said, "I hope you realize how difficult it is to *get* good scuppernong these days! Don't drink all of it, please." As no one paid him any mind, whatsoever, he said it again, louder. And since it became perfectly obvious, then, that none of these pirates cared a fig how difficult it was to get good scuppernong these days—or about anything else, at the moment—Merchanty Swift slipped into the night and away, leaving the pirates to the fearful heats of their own avarice and excess.

While the Prudence Committee waited for Merchanty Swift to be found (which, of course, he wouldn't be, just yet, would he?) Opportune Baggs The Inventor wished to bring up one or two technical matters. By a slight rearrangement of components which he and his family had brought with them, he said, he believed an instrument could be constructed which would enable a scouting party to signal the main body without making any unwholesome squeaks—or any noises of any kind, for that matter. He was well into a rather complex description of the signaling instrument and, at the actual moment of interruption, had digressed only briefly to explain why an earlier version of the device had failed. It seems that (in the earlier version) he had forgot one of the basic laws of mousephysics. He should have known better, he said in his usual self-effacing manner, but, as he was self-taught in these things, he confessed to a certain lack of discipline. He thought, in fact, that this might be a characteristic distinction between inventors, say, and true scientists.

It was just here that Kneebuckle Tweeks skittered directly through the midst of the convened Prudence Committee at work.

The committeemice stared after Master Tweeks for a moment, dumbfounded at such shocking manners, and, I don't doubt, considering whether to comment upon the pass to which things had come with young mice these days. But, before any of them could decide to say anything about anything, Clickety Whatstraw came right behind him—only faster. She in turn was followed by Hazeltine Smarts and Lookety Twoflutes practically tumbling over one another in their haste.

General Random Chewings stood up. "Here, here!" he said. But it was ineffective. Thistles Whitefoot actually bumped into him as he was saying it, dislodging a plume from the General's bicorne. While young Whitefoot, much to his credit, was on tiptoe in a strenuous attempt to restore the plume to its rightful place on a very impressive hat, old Teeters McGnaw, with a firkin of oatmeal stout on his shoulder, plowed into them both and before any plumes could be replaced or uniforms straightened or teacups put away, Peterson Crinkles and Pendleton Needleteeth, not to mention the oatmeal stout, were all over them in a heap. On top of all of *them* then, in an instant, were Wickersham Pickers, Weaverly Pleats, three more of the Twoflutes and at least two of the Threepurples. There were mice absolutely everywhere! Hungerford Pinks and Predicate Quoty, Nibbles Entoo, and on top of them, at one point, Holcomb Peepers! (If I do not mistake, Mr. E. E. Asquith-Berryseed III, himself, actually turned up somewhere in this group. He was, as I remember, immediately helping the others and not at all attending to his own dignity. One could have imagined a lot worse from a mouse carrying the burden of a name like that!)

But there were many more: Warburton Nines Who Once Lifted A Cat; Twitterton Scoops; Old Miss Middlechippers; Farnaby Pockets and his mother, who, between them, inadvertently knocked over the Mayor, who, while he was being stood up and brushed off, noticed Proserpine Pockets in a NEW WAY and was thereafter unable easily to recall why he had wanted to be a bachelor in the first place; young Crinoline Fluflax, who, in the kerfuffle, had somehow misplaced all four of the cucumber sandwiches her mother had packed for her—which she had so looked forward to eating!—and was just thinking to herself that she had not been this disappointed since Whistles Morehouse aimed to kiss her during spelling and missed; Wrinkles Freestone carrying that old canary yellow slatback rocker which had been whittled from the dry root of a blown-down lombardy poplar by his great-uncle Hammersmith Pipes during some cold and dreary January days long ago and painted early that February by his great-aunt Honeysuckle Pipes, who had always thought a couple coats of canary yellow would cheer up just about anything no matter what month of the year it was.

And they *kept* coming: Umpteen Weeks; the Lickerbees; the Chewlingfords; Quicklesmith Peets, who would make you some bang-up cherry pickles if you brought him the cherry; Teegarten Nutbutters and his mice. I simply couldn't tell you who all came through there: several of the Whiskersons, I know that; the Shredder girls; Lintsaver Creeples. They were all running and bumping and falling down and getting back up and saying desperate things such as "I beg your pardon" and "Oops!" and "Sorry about your biscuit." It was awful! Not AT ALL what one wanted.

CHAPTER 24

What Happened at the Bottom
of the Steep Decline

Be that as it may, and whether one wanted it or not, The Hesitation at Lawn's End was now essentially complete. All that remained was for the Prudence Committee to wake Sir Rotherham—as gently as possible under the circumstances—gather up teacups and run for their lives. They joined the rest of the company in an expeditious, if disorganized, trip down the steep decline toward the unknown and away from the known—the known being the shape of A Large Yellowish and Stripy Cat silhouetted against the moon.

The steep decline was a problem. It became steeper, you see—quite a lot steeper—until near the bottom it was more like what one might call a cliff. And, too, you must picture that the descenders down it were lugging great bits of impedimenta—all sorts of it: grips and pouches and bags and pokes and packs and sacks and cartons and crates, to say nothing of trunks and valises and hampers and scuttles and boxes and lockers and portmanteaus. And I should tell you, incidentally, that most of these items never reached the bottom at all. In terror of their lives the mice simply let go their loads

and covered their eyes as they disappeared over the cliff—
some of them at amazing speeds! But, wonderfully, at the very
bottom of all this was a considerable amount of water. It was
just ploop ploop plop ploop for the longest time.

And things being as they are—again, wonderfully—field
mice are apparently instinctive little swimmers or thrashers
or flailers or whatever you might call the thing which they
did in the water. Never having done it before, they somehow
did it now, and, albeit shaken and somewhat surprised, they
all eventually found themselves on the little beach at the base
of the cliff where there was the awfullest amount of cough-
ing and sneezing and nose blowing followed by nearly as
much wringing of wet fur and squibbing about in one's ears
and padding about on the soft mud trying to find one's rel-
atives. The children thought it enormous fun and nobody
got any sleep of any kind whatsoever, of
course, but, in the end, these mice
just shook themselves as
dry as possible and hugged
one other and counted
themselves happy to be
uneaten and each of
them more or less in
one piece.

It was just here,
on the little beach
at the base of the
cliff, that Merchanty
Swift rejoined the

company and began immediately to ask whether anyone had seen Grenadine Fieldpea and was she all right. They had and she was.

Now. I have, from time to time, gone to some lengths, in this account, to point it out that field mice do not gossip. But let us be honest and straightforward. If certain of the field mice of Tottensea did *not* gossip about this event, then I don't know how the word is to be defined. But it was an extraordinary thing, wasn't it? And perhaps allowances can be made. In any event, and whether allowances can be made or not, I am here compelled to say that knowledge of this small happening—the asking, by one mouse, whether anyone had seen a particular other mouse and was she all right— was disseminated throughout Tottensea with electrical speed, and was, moreover, accompanied by substantial commentary!

But, on a night of extraordinary events, there was more. For on this night and at this place—here, at the bottom of the steep decline—Tottensea looked up. First, a few of them, then more of them, and, at length, all of them looked up. UP!

For most of them, it was their first time, ever, out and away from The Cottage and its lights, and, more particularly, away from its security light. The security light was a very modern and up-to-date electrical thing erected against burglars and other terrors of the dark and the mice had lived their lives under it. Every single night it burned . . . and *all* night, too—burned with a half-light that had robbed them of the night sky.

But here, away from the blindness of half-light, they had

got it back! And it was wondrous. Here all Tottensea stood, homeless, damp, looking up and transfixed by this new and resplendent sky: black and velvet and radiant with the most exquisite jewelry—more stars than ever they had imagined spread across the whole heavens! They were speechless.

Old Umpteen Weeks, of a sudden, seemed to remember something and was uncharacteristically beside himself with ecstasy. He danced feebly around his cane and all of Tottensea was somehow with him in his joy—though why, they did not know. They did not know that a new kind of happiness was on its way to them, that—much more than stars!—a whole world of lost birthright would now be restored to them.

They would come to know that they were, indeed, meant to be out here, just as the Mayor had said. Something untried or forgot would awaken in them, something acute and keen, something effortless and unlearned—something *given* to them. It was coursing through them even now, stirring from long sleeps the rightful drives and cautions and curiosities. The noses of Tottensea, long dulled by some domestic tameness in their air, would awaken to exotic tangs and flavors, sharp and pure and piquant. Whiskers, grown languid and cosmetic with disuse, would soon twitch usefully, with significance.

The lush richness of the meadow would uplift them, invigorate their lives and furbish their arts, too. The glory of waving field and tumbling brook would animate their music and dance, the brilliance of wildflower rouse their senses and vivify their canvases. Their poetry would rise up, borne away from sweet affectations and literary conceits, toward the pungent tartness of real things. It would be splendid!

Of course . . . anything could happen out here! There would be dangers, yes—hawks and owls, weasels, even, and foxes. But with the dangers there would be fresh quickenings, a new cunning. The half-light was gone from their eyes and they could see right well into the new night—soon they would be confident there, canny and full of craft. Even now they felt more ready and alert. More nimble. More fleet.

CHAPTER 25

The New Day

The new day dawned on such an assortment as you've never seen of mousestockings and other less mentionable things laid out to dry on any pebble or sprig of grass which could be pressed into service. And as field mice are both modest *and* considerate there was ever so much looking straight ahead and minding one's own business throughout the morning.

As for those burdens which had been dropped before going over the cliff—a climb back up the slope (after having located a much more gradual route than that by which they had descended!) revealed a disheartening sight: mousebelongings. Mousebelongings everywhere! In every state of disarray, too: baggage broken open, contents spilled out, strewn, scattered, trampled, soiled and mixed up with other mice's things as you could hardly believe.

Most of the books had been dropped right there, on the slope, and some of them were soiled. But at least they hadn't plopped into the water, everyone said. You could sell a soiled book, Glendowner Fieldpea told them—discounting it, of course, as you would certainly have to do. But no amount of discounting would be of the least help once a book had gone into the drink, he said.

And, of course, Thurgood Fidgetson's book *had* gone into the drink. Or, at least, Thurgood *Fidgetson* had gone into the drink. And here was the most amazing thing. The book came out bone dry! Thurgood's sense of responsibility, here, and his remarkable achievement in this connection became something of a Tottensea legend and Mr. Fieldpea determined to memorialize it in some appropriate way, eventually, when things had settled down a little.

A saying came out of it. Mice will say (I have heard them), "Do you have anything to drink? I'm as dry as Thurgood Fidgetson's book!" Sometimes they will say, "I'm as dry as Thurgood Fidgetson's poetry." But that's hardly fair to Thurgood, is it? *He* didn't write the poetry! And it wasn't the poetry that was dry, in any event. It was the book. But they do say that.

Anyway, it was certainly a mess, that slope. And for creatures as orderly and particular as field mice . . . Well, it was a trial. That's all there is to it. But along with all their troubles they had this comfort: The Cat was nowhere to be seen.

And so to work. It took them all the livelong day and in spite of their best efforts it was simply too dangerous to move some of the larger items down the slope. For even

though the slope of their new route was more gradual, it wasn't *that* gradual! But Opportune Baggs The Inventor was there and, seeing what had to be done, he called for his family. After a bit of thought and some rough sketches he took the elliptical conjoiner of the nib stabilizer which Parnassus had been carrying and attached it in such a way that while it lay actually athwart Lavinia's nonsequential parchment circumventor, it nevertheless continued to subtend the arc described by Maximillian's intersecting ankle mitigator—and that was the key! It wasn't perfect, of course, but it *did work* and with it they lowered the large items down the cliff with only a few skittery thuds and splats and no loss of life whatsoever.

And as for the body of water which they had all fallen into, when the General got a good look at it, at first light, he actually whistled. "It's an absolute sea if ever I've seen one!" Which, of course, he hadn't. And it wasn't. He had, nevertheless, read about seas in certain naval treatises and things and this was exactly how he pictured them. "Water to the right. Water to the left. Water straight ahead. That, my friends, is a sea" is how he put it. But as to what one does with a sea, once one has identified it . . . that was another matter altogether. He remembered, in a general way, about frigates and galleons and dreadnoughts and words like that, but mousebook illustrations being simply not very good in the early days when he studied naval affairs, he found himself, here, squinting into the morning mist with only the vaguest notion of what kind of maritime shapes he might be trying to recognize. In the end he didn't see anything except . . . well, for a brief moment he thought he might have seen a frog looking at him. But, then, seas don't have frogs, do they? No, of course not. Ponds have frogs. Weirs have frogs. Rivers even have frogs. Seas do not have frogs.

Unlike the General, however, all the little mouselings in the company knew exactly what one does with a sea or a pond or a river or whatever it was they had fallen into. One gets in it. The irresistible nature of this intuitive knowledge was pointed up by the quiet, somewhat staccato and businesslike instructions of various of their mothers which punctuated the morning's activities: "Friday Threepurples, get away from that water and stay away from it, do you understand?" and of course, he got away from that water and stayed away from it, or "Get back from there, Pepper Quicksnip, and I do mean now!" and he got back from there and did it right then, or "Lemuel Twitchings, come right here and away from that water and don't make me say it again," and he came right there and away from that water and didn't make her say it again. (Technically, she would not have said it again. Field mice only give one warning.)

Now if this type of exhortation appears unduly sharp or out of character for these normally soft-spoken and excellent little mothers, well . . . it isn't. While it *is* true that none of them had ever imagined such a thing as this much water in one place and while it *is* true that such a thing was frightening to them, it is *not* true that they were being cross. They were being what a field mouse would have called "firm" or "clear."

And I would have you understand that the little mice were obedient not because they were naturally good children (there are no such things—not among field mice, at least) but because they had been trained, you see. They knew that if they did not do what they were told they would be punished, and that right quickly. I can promise you that not a single one of those three boys was thinking—when he obeyed—about any dangers in the water or about how these instructions were for his own good. He was only thinking he didn't want to be spanked! I can promise you, further, that this was a much smaller burden for a little heart to carry than some enormous consideration such as what really was out there in the water or what was, in some long run, for one's own good. And since smaller burdens make for lighter hearts, those boys were soon playing happily on the beach and not thinking of the water very much at all. Way down in their little mouse-bones, you see, they knew something they didn't even know they knew. They knew that if it had been all right to play in the water they *could* have played in the water. Or, if you like, we could put that another way: they knew that their mothers loved them.

But about midmorning something began to change. If you had been there you could have seen that it was changing because a few of the mothers began to wade a little way out into the water, testing the bottom cautiously as they went. Other mothers climbed up onto some of the various field-stones scattered around the beach or into accessible crannies of the cliff, from which places they looked very searchingly out into the water, all the while (those who weren't wearing bonnets) shading their eyes from the morning sun with a paw or perhaps with two paws. And well before noon those good children got their day in the water.

And what a day it was. Why, you would have thought it

was the most wonderful holiday in the world. Such squeals and shrieks of laughter and such drenchings and splurtings and splashings they did! The mothers didn't have quite as much fun, of course, as they were looking and watching and hoping that those really *were* frogs and not something much worse looking back at them from way out there in the water. But they took turns. They weren't all watching all the time. Sometimes, some of them were building fires for roasting marshmallows over or trying to find dry towels or making sandwiches. By dark, nevertheless, they were all very tired mothers and some of them may have felt a trifle anxious, but the *children,* you see, were perfectly happy and not at all aware that they were poor little emigrants to be pitied because they didn't have homes. They didn't worry about things like that. They just put their heads down wherever their mothers told them to put their heads down and fell fast asleep in a mouseminute. Or less.

EPILOGUE

So it came to be that Tottensea went out. And they are out there still! They wouldn't be pleased if I told you *just* where they are, of course, for they are hidden. And so they must remain or be in peril of their lives. They do have enemies, you know.

They are a bit different, now, in the way they do things. But of course they would be, wouldn't they? There are no compost heaps out there, you see. And they don't pinch things from anyone's vegetable garden, either. They have learnt to be field mice—and are all the more delightful for it, in my opinion.

They have discovered a world of foods that were meant for them and for which they are devising superb new recipes to this very day. Merchanty Swift still brings in wonderful things from afar, of course (they *will* want their cheeses and chocolate!) and has begun a lively commerce exporting some of the exotic delicacies which they have found in the fields. It turns out that there are tubers which certain creatures simply won't be without once they have been introduced to them. I am not free to tell you the names of these, as the field mice consider that to be proprietary information.

The New Bookish Mouse is smaller than the old one. There's a plaque on the door:

Though small,
we are
(it is to be hoped)
devoted to quality.

It's true, actually. They are. And I should probably point out that, although The New Bookish Mouse *is* a bit smaller than the old one, there is a special wing adjoining it called The Thurgood Fidgetson Memorial Lending Library. There, the most farthingless mouse can borrow a book, absolutely free, for up to two weeks—even longer, if it's a very large book and he makes special arrangements. Some of the books are soiled, yes, but they are nonetheless entirely readable.

And I should also tell you that there are some very nice new volumes—recently written—and more coming, as I'm told. The following is a partial list, annotated:

Farnaby and the Pirates
by Grenadine Swift
A true account. Based on actual interviews. Thrilling.

Teaching Penmanship in the Schools—a Plea
by Octavia Baggs
A commonsense approach. Some shocking examples shown.

Why I Gave Up Writing Poetry
by Adverbial Quoty
Earnest and well-meaning, but, on the whole, not well written.

Adjustment: The Key to Things
by Opportune Baggs
Mice, life, and machinery. Thought-provoking. Runs on a bit.

The Mousewriter and Its Uses
by Opportune Baggs
A handbook of Mousewriter adjustments, settings and accessories. Chapter titles include:
- Preparing Legal Documents and Party Invitations
- Automatic Knitting and Grape Peeling
- The Steam Calliope Option
- Straightening Teeth with the Mousewriter

Living with Politics
by Proserpine Carryforth
Helpful guidelines from the Mayor's wife. Tips on bucking a mouse up, watching his weight and assisting with wisdom.

Field Mouse Armies, Sea Frogs and Other Things That Are Not
by Random Chewings
A humorous journey of self-discovery. All about paying attention to things that *are.* Entertaining.

The Colonel and the Scullery Maid
by Clementine Chewings
True love and tons of difficulty. A good cry if a bit thick. Fiction.

On Not Overheating—the Proper Limits of Excitement
by Farnaby Pockets

A young mouse's reflections on the joys of calming down. Informative sections on crossword puzzles, beetle watching, and not jumping off high things without permission.

To Love Again
by Merchanty Swift
A brief volume of poetry. Well-metered and -rhymed, we thought. Romantic.

So that's it, then. We shall leave Tottensea just there, I think—writing books and buying them or, if they can't afford that, borrowing them—and being generally happy in their new life. This tale is done.

My purpose being accomplished, then, I must take my leave of you, dear reader. I have grown quite fond of you, as it happens, and I hope it won't be thought forward of me to go on thinking of you as a friend. With your permission, then:

> *So here's to you, my friend*
> *I bid farewell—and hail!*
> *Good listener you have been*
> *To this poor linnet's tale.*

There. I'm off. You must surely have other things to do than be forever listening to some bird going on about field mice, after all. And, taking the long view, I have things to be about, as well. Spring *is* coming, isn't it?